The Chi

To.
Anne

Ira Hughes

Ira Hughes

The Christmas Bell
Copyright©2001 Ira Hughes

Printed in the United States of America

CEDAR HILL PRESS
P.O. BOX 235
Knightstown, IN 46148

ISBN 0-9713981-0-0

This book is dedicated to my grandchildren,
Brandie, Noah, Casie.
You make my heart sing

Acknowledgments

My husband, Gerald, who crafted the bell for the cover.
Jan Hughes for reading, editing and editing again.
Ruth Ann Rains for listening, reading and editing.
Lynda McClellan for her encouragement.

Chapter One

On her deathbed my mother whispered to me, *"The bell, Taylor. The bell holds the secret, the secret of who you really are."* Before I could ask what she was talking about, she took one last breath and was gone. "Wait. Please wait," I'd begged, staring at the cancer-ravaged body. But it was too late, whatever she could have told me, forever silenced.

Today, after the service,--Mother had made me promise there would be no calling and only a graveside service-- and the family members and friends are gone, I stand at the front window of the large Victorian house I grew up in and stare out across the massive lawn, with its huge maple trees, bare now in the December twilight. The streetlights are coming on, soft amber. Brownbell Avenue is the oldest section of Scalesville. Only the wealthiest families lived on this avenue during the early part of the 20th century. And wealthy families still live here. We were wealthy once.

I feel the silence of the house and suddenly realize it had always been quiet, like it had a need all its own and demanded that the occupants be hushed.

Out by Thursday, the foreclosure notice said. How many had the bank sent before that final one? Poor Mother.

The doctors said the cancer killed my mother and that it was too far-gone before they found it. But I don't believe that is how it happened at all. I believe Marcus Conrad killed her, killed her just as surely as if he'd put a gun to her head. She was a proud woman, my mother. And she couldn't live with the shame of it all.

Marcus Conrad was a charmer, a snake in the grass, like you see on those newsmagazines on television. He'd breezed into town, told my mother what she wanted to hear, and in just months had convinced her to put up everything she owned as collateral on a *"can't fail"* business deal. A few months later, he was gone, and she was getting foreclosure notices from the bank. Just last week, I heard he'd been found dead of a heart attack as he'd tried to woo another unsuspecting lonely woman. It turned out he'd left a string of broken women all over the country. Most were too ashamed to press charges.

I'd taken a leave from my job, as art teacher in Parkview Junior High in Cincinnati, and had come home to Scalesville to care for my mother. Now, here I am on this gray December day with just a few hundred dollars in my bank account, my four-year old Ford Taurus, and a notice that the property must be vacated by next Thursday. And I don't know what to do. Go back to Cincinnati? They are holding my job, but I have no real home there either. The lease on my apartment had been up, and instead of renewing it, I'd stored my belongings. I'd thought my mother had maybe a few weeks. As it turned out she had only days.

I laid my face against the coolness of the thick glass on the front door of the home that I'd grown up in. It should have been mine. But did I really want it? I close my eyes and try to bring forth a warm memory of growing up here. I search my brain until it aches; still I can't find what I've been looking for my whole life. Sure, the house had been filled with things, wonderful things, but there was always something missing.

The first floor is barren of all furniture. The rental company came last week and took it away. Mother had sold most of her old furniture and rented new, it was what Marcus had wanted, telling her that she could redecorate anytime she wanted. She saved a few pieces, storing them in the attic, and she'd kept the furniture in my old bedroom. Don't think I really want any of the furniture that's in the attic, maybe store my bedroom things, maybe just leave what's in the attic for the new owners.

Again, my mother's words echo across my brain. "The bell, Taylor. The bell holds the secret of who you really are."

Who I really am? I'd wondered about that countless times. When I was eight, my parents told me I was adopted. No details. Just that Grandmother Winfield had brought me home from a foster care place when I was three months old. Learning that I was adopted had explained why my auburn hair wasn't dark like my father's, nor blonde like my mother's. Back then, Mother's hair had been a natural silken blonde. As the years went by, she'd kept it that way with the help of her hairdresser.

A couple of times, I'd tried to ask about the people who had given me away. My mother had been infuriated that I would ask. Besides there was nothing to tell. After all didn't I have a great home, the best of everything? Why would I even want to know?

Yes, I had all that. Still, it hurt to the core of my soul that my first parents had given me away. How could anyone do that, just throw their own flesh and blood away? Sometimes, growing up, I'd find myself just staring into the mirror in my room. I'd look deep into my green eyes and try to see something of who I really was. What were those people whose eyes I'd inherited, like? Did a thought of a thrown away baby girl ever cross their minds?

My father died when I was ten, leaving my mother and me well provided for. Now that she was gone, was there any way to find out, at least the names of the people, who had given me away? I could go on the Internet into one of those search for people places. My laptop is in the storage bin in Cincinnati. I could go to the library. But to search I would have to have a name, maybe even a place. The only close relative is Aunt Kate, my mother's older sister by two years. They had married brothers---sons of a domineering woman, Harriet Winfield.

Would Aunt Kate know anything about the bell? I walk into the parlor and pick up the phone, thankful that the phone company

3

hadn't disconnected, else I'd have to use my cell phone. I sank to the floor. My knees are trembling. I'd always been a little afraid of Aunt Kate. When I was a child she was forever telling me to stand up straight, and stop running. "Hello," she answers curtly on the third ring.

"Aunt Kate, this is Taylor," I said as firmly as I could make my voice speak.

"Is everything all right, Taylor?" she asks. I think she fears that I'll be asking for something. She knows about my mother losing everything.

"Yes, Aunt Kate. Everything is fine. I just want to ask you something."

"Yes."

"Do you know the names of the people who gave me up for adoption?" I say it all fast and wait.

For a long moment there is total silence on the other end of the line, then a heavy sigh. "Taylor, don't go trying to dig all that up. It would be best to just forget about it."

Forget! I bite my lip to keep from screaming. How could I forget? All this is part of who I am. To forget would be to let part of me die. "Please, Aunt Kate. Do you know their names? Are there records? Surely there were adoption records."

"Taylor, I'm afraid all you are going to do is upset yourself by probing into all this. You had parents who provided well for you. I don't understand why you are wanting more than that. Frankly, I think it's disrespectful to their memory to try to find those people who gave you up."

People who gave you up. The words sting, but I press on. "Aunt Kate, I know my parents provided well for me, and I'm grateful for all they did for me. But this has nothing to do with them. It only has to do with me. Now, my records? Do you know anything about my records?"

"Taylor, all the records were burned."

"What? There was a fire?"

"Your grandmother Winfield burned your records the day you came into that house."

4

"Why? Why would Grandmother Winfield do that? What right did she have to do that!" My voice is rising, trembling.

"She thought it best that all ties were severed. And to prevent something just like you are trying to do from happening. Just let it go, Taylor. For your own good, and in respect for the memory of your parents, just let it go."

Hot tears choke my throat. What right did others have to decide for me what was best, what should be let go?

Then I remember my mother's last words. "Aunt Kate, do you know anything about a bell?

"Bell?"

"Mother whispered to me just before she died that the secret of where I came from is with a bell."

"Good God! Wasn't that burned along with the records?"

My heart is racing. "There really was a bell! You know about it? You know what she meant by the bell holding the secret!" You have to tell me, Aunt Kate. Please tell me! Tell me what Mother was talking about!"

"Mother Winfield would turn over in her grave if she knew your mother saved the bell."

"Where is the Bell?" I'm almost shouting into the phone. "Where did my mother put the bell?"

"I don't know, Taylor. I didn't even know she'd kept it.

"But, you did see it. Didn't you? What did it look like?"

"Yes, I saw it."

I close my eyes and wait, praying that she'd remember enough to describe it, that she'd care enough to describe it.

"It was a little craft thing."

"What?"

"You know, handmade. Like you'd find in a craft shop. It was made out of wood, painted. And it was strange. It had been cut down the middle, in a zigzag cut. And there was really only half of it in the envelope."

"An envelope? Was there a message inside?"

"Not that I saw. I wonder how Caroline managed to keep Mother Winfield from knowing she'd kept it out? If she actually did," Aunt Kate adds almost in a whisper."

"Thank you for telling me this, Aunt Kate."

"Well, I don't like it one bit, you probing into all this. I don't know how you are going to find out anything. And how will you know you'll like what you find, even if you turn up something?"

"I only want to know who they are. Where I came from. I believe in the end that Mother understood my needing to know. Why else would she have told me about the bell?"

My aunt sighs loudly. "Caroline was terribly sick there at the end. Taylor, you know she came and went. Maybe she was talking out of her head, confused."

"I don't feel that. I think she sensed how much it meant to me. I think the bell is somewhere in this house."

"Even if you find it, what good will it do you?"

I didn't tell my aunt that it would be like touching a part of who I am. I just said, "Thanks again, Aunt Kate."

My aunt warns me again about trying to dig up things that are better left buried.

After we hang up, I just sit there in the shadows, wondering how people who have always known where they came from, can so freely tell those of us who have wondered since they were eight years old that it is best to *forget it*? Do they really listen to their words?

I remind myself there was a chance that Aunt Kate was right, that Mother was talking out of her head. But her voice had been so clear. *"The bell, Taylor. The bell holds the secret."*

If she had indeed kept the bell, why had she done it, defying Grandmother Winfield? I like to think she sensed that in a future time the little baby she had taken to raise as her own would need it. What had she really been like, this woman who had taken a baby, not her own, into this huge house? Maybe I hadn't known her at all. Perhaps I had been a constant reminder of her own little girl that she could never have. Maybe adopting a baby hadn't been her idea at

6

all, nor my father's. I suspect that Grandmother Winfield had been the one in charge of it all. Grandmother Winfield died when I was eight, about a month before I was told that I was adopted.

Aunt Kate had said that the bell was homemade. I teach art. Had the person who sent the bell with a baby been artistic? Was there a connection? But why had it been cut in two? Aunt Kate's words thunder across my brain, *"How do you know you will like what you might find?"* A shiver runs across my shoulders. Suppose I found that I have sadistic genes? Could I handle something like that? So much to consider. Maybe I shouldn't try to find out. Maybe just go through life feeling as if part of me was missing. I quickly discard that thought. I couldn't do that. I'll just have to start from ground zero and deal with it as it comes. The not knowing is worse than anything I could possibly find out.

Where to look? Had my mother tucked it into a nook or cranny? In the attic or basement? The attic! Of course. In all the old movies weren't all secrets kept in the attic? I jump as the doorbell rings. I don't want to see anyone. I stand up, ease to the front window and look out. Libby. She rings the bell again, then begins pounding on the door. "Taylor. Open up, Taylor. I know you're in there!"

I flip on the porch light and open the door to my best friend since second grade. "What are you doing, making enough noise to wake the whole neighborhood?"

She gives me a quick hug. "And what are you doing in a dark house? I feared they'd turned your electric off already." Libby knew about the financial troubles of my mother; I suspect that everyone in Scalesville knows.

"I just hadn't turned the lights on yet. Come on in." I flip the foyer light on. "Come on back to the kitchen and I'll make tea," I said, flipping on lights as we make our way to the back of the house.

Elizabeth (Libby to all of us who love her and that is almost everyone who knows her) Mills Cornwallis is absolutely the happiest person I have ever known. Once I asked her why she was so happy. *"Because I choose to be,"* she'd said, looking at me as if wondering why I didn't choose so wisely.

Anyway, Libby's plan for her life had been to grow up, go to college, marry Jason Cornwallis, the boy two houses down the street from her, have three children, two boys and a girl, and live happily ever after. So far she's right on target. She'd gone to college, majoring in home economics, married the man of her dreams, and has twin boys. All she lacks is the little girl. I don't doubt she'll get that as well.

As I put the water on to boil, Libby sits on one of the four bar stools--didn't belong to the rental company--and asks, "What do you hear from Alex?"

"He called after Mother died asking if there was anything he could do."

"Do you ever wish things had turned out differently?"

I really don't want to talk about Alex, but don't tell her so. "It turned out for the best, Libby," I said, turning to look at my slender, blue-eyed friend. "He's got someone in Seattle, and I'm glad for him."

"Really?"

"Really," I smile at her.

"But you two were so right for each other."

"In your eyes, Libby. The truth is, we both found out that what we had was not a lifetime thing, not like you and Jason. Are you still going home tomorrow?" I asked, wanting to change the subject.

"Yes. The boys and I will be on the 7.A.M flight. Jason calls two, three times a day. We miss each other terribly. A week apart is pure torture for both of us. But it was my Dad's birthday, and I had to be here. Jason couldn't get away; the firm is working on a big case right now."

"You are truly happy, just the way you planned," I tell her as I pour our tea.

"Of course," she said. "I believe if you want something badly enough, you can make it happen. And you know I wanted Jason since I was a little girl." She giggles, "Of course he wanted me just as much."

I stare at her, wondering if I had her strong willpower, the total belief in making what you want in life happen, if I had just a spark of what she had, could I find my roots?

"What?" Libby asks, realizing that I'm just staring at her. "Something big is on your mind. Come on. Tell me. You didn't find a dream man in Cincinnati and keep it a secret, did you?" She grabs my wrists. "Tell all, Taylor. Keep no secrets from me." She waits, her bright blue eyes dancing with excitement, to hear about some man who is going to make my life as happy as her own. I smile. Everything happiness to her involved a prince charming and a princess waiting for him to find her and carry her away to a dream castle, where life was happy ever after.

I sigh and tell my friend about my mother's last words, and what Aunt Kate had told me about seeing the bell. I tell her it was made of wood, but I don't tell about it being cut in two, although, I don't know exactly why I leave that out.

Libby's mouth flies open. "Wow, Taylor. A mystery. A better than a novel mystery. It's all so exciting. What if you find out you came from royalty or something like that, and the bell is a family crest? Maybe you were stolen and they have been waiting all these years for your return." Libby is off the barstool, her hands flying with excitement. "And the bell, Taylor. The bell will prove that you are the long lost princess!"

I have to laugh. "Libby, I swear, you have the wildest imagination."

"Anything is possible, Taylor."

"Yeah," I said, remembering the thought about sadistic genes that had flashed across my mind when Aunt Kate had told me about the bell being cut in two.

"You have to find that bell. You just have to," Libby said, sitting back down on the barstool. "I can't believe that you haven't already torn this place apart, looking for it."

"I only found out a little while ago from Aunt Kate that there actually was a bell."

"Well, come on!" Libby says, jumping off the stool. "Where do we start to look?"

In that moment, I realize if I do find the bell, I don't want to share its discovery with anyone, not even this dearest friend. "I'm just going to wait until tomorrow to start looking."

"Darn! Why don't you want to start right away? I could help."

"You need to go back to your parents' house and spend time with them. I'll bet you aren't even packed, and your plane leaves early tomorrow."

Libby sighs, then grins. "You're right. I have to pack. You know me, always waiting until the last minute. And I do want to spend a few moments tonight with Mom and Dad. But you call and tell me when you find the bell."

"Ok," I promised. Not reminding her there is a chance there isn't a bell at all; that it was most likely burned up with all the other links to my past just like Aunt Kate said. I don't like to think about that possibility. It leaves me feeling hollow inside.

After Libby left, I went upstairs to bed. Mother hadn't changed anything in my room, although she'd redecorated most every other room in the house just like Marcus had wanted. The thought that she had cared for me, although she had seemed distant and cold, gave me a sad comfort.

I stare at the wall across from my bed. Shadows, from the giant maple tree outside, dance across its surface. Some of my earliest memories are of shadows on that wall. In summer when leaves covered the branches, the shadows looked like fluffy, doll clothes swinging on a clothesline. And in winter the shadows had the old people's knotty hands. The shadows have the winter hands now. I'd been afraid the first time I saw the shadows. It had been the knotty hands. I'd cried out. Mother had come into the room, telling me to "Sh" and to go back to sleep. I'd covered my head and hugged the stuffed, brown teddy I'd named Boo. Grandmother Winfield took Boo away when I was five. She said he was old, ragged and dirty. She replaced him with a clean new teddy, she named Bear. Bear still sits over there on my shelf. He may have become old, but he never became ragged and dirty.

As I listen to the wind swaying the branches ever so lightly, I

10

wonder about the bell. Has it really been waiting all these years for me to find? I fold my hands behind my head and just lie there with my eyes wide open. I can't help smiling as I recall what Libby had said about the bell possibly being a royalty crest, and me being stolen. Libby should have been a writer.

Chapter Two

I awaken to wind-tossed rain splattering against the windowpane. I let my eyes adjust to the gray light of a rainy December morning.

I get out of bed and stand at the window. The streetlights are still on, and will be on all day if the grayness doesn't lighten up. Old man Hubbard, across the street, hobbles off his porch and picks up a soggy newspaper from the step. Wonder how old he is? He'd hobbled like that when I'd been a child. Most of the kids in the neighborhood were afraid of him. Libby wasn't. She said that he was actually a witch's husband and when the witch put children in her oven, he always freed them.

I glance at my watch: seven-thirty. Libby should be on her way home by now. The only part of Libby's life-plan that hadn't happened was that I'd be living next door to her with my own prince charming and three kids. I don't recall dreaming about a prince charming for myself. Sure I'd wanted someone special, someone who thought I was special, too. But I had wanted an equal partner in life, not someone who was a rock, protecting a tiny stone. Maybe for a few weeks there I'd thought Alex fit what I wanted. He was handsome and kind, and for awhile, physical attraction was enough. I'm thankful we both realized that physical attraction was all we shared. He'd moved to Seattle, knew a friend who loved it there, and took with him the girl from the athletic department. I wish him the happiness I don't think we could ever have found. After Alex left, I'd dated now and then. Never met anyone I wanted to see more than twice.

I go down the hall and push open the door to my mother's bedroom, the room she'd shared with Marcus, the room with the best view. Had she felt loved in this room? God, I hope so. I don't think the bell could possibly be in here, had ever been in this room. The closet? I rush across the room, pull open the closet door and flip on the light. Bare. What had I expected? A box with a piece of who I am sitting on the shelf? I turn off the light and walk across the room. This had once been Grandmother Winfield's room. It suddenly feels cold. I quickly exit the room, pulling the door closed behind me.

After my shower I dress in gray sweats. It's raining harder now, and I turn on lights as I go downstairs. I start a pot of coffee, then put a strawberry pop tart in the toaster.

As I chew the half-burnt pastry, my thoughts are on the day ahead. Where to start my search? I suddenly realize that I'm stalling. Why hadn't I ripped this place apart last night after Aunt Kate told me that a bell had actually existed? "I'm afraid," I say aloud, realizing I'd been afraid I wouldn't find anything and the dream of finding my origins would be gone. By not looking, I could hold on to the dream. If I looked and nothing was there, the dream died. Stop this nonsense thinking I tell myself, licking the last bit of strawberry off my finger, and decide that the attic would be where I'd start my search.

I go upstairs, open the door to the stairway leading to the attic and pull on the dangling string, turning on the single light bulb in the stairway. I climb the stairs till I'm standing on the attic floor. As a child, I'd played up here. It was here I read "Flowers in the Attic", a book I don't think was intended for an eleven-year-old. For months afterwards, I'd stayed out of here. I flip the light switch, turning on the light bulb dangling by a cord from a rafter.

I scan the entire attic. Two gray overstuffed chairs, turned legs up, lie on a table with huge carved legs; several pieces of antiques: dressers, tables and lamps, which I suppose had belonged to past generations of Winfields. Many boxes line one wall. A mannequin stands alone near the window. I remember putting old dresses on it as a child. A small writing desk sits on the other side of the window. All in all, I guess there really isn't much here. Not at all cluttered like Libby's attic, where she said a fairy princess had once been held captive for a whole year, of course Prince Charming had rescued her. Was there a piece of a wooden bell, linking me to people with auburn hair, lying somewhere within my reach?

I pull the top box from a stack of four. I open the box. It

13

contains a set of crystal wrapped in newspapers from 1947. I guess this belonged to Grandmother Winfield. Maybe all the things in this attic belonged to her. I stare at the writing desk. Suddenly a memory of when I'd been about four: I'd gone into my mother's bedroom. Had this been the desk that was sitting in front of her bedroom window? I close my eyes and try to see it all, just as I'd seen it that long ago day. Yes, it had been this desk. I'd begun playing with my mother's writing pens. I can see so plainly the ivory knob, with a tiny rose sketched on the surface, on the drawer in the center of the desk. I actually see my small hand opening the drawer. Why had I not remembered that? Why was the memory so vivid now? I see myself, my tiny hand pulling on the drawer, pulling it open. There had been an envelope inside. I'd taken my forefinger and run it along the flap. I'd gotten a glimpse of what was inside. Just a flash of color, vivid red. Just then Grandmother Winfield and my mother had appeared at the door. *"What are you doing?"* Grandmother had sternly demanded. *"You aren't allowed to play in here!"* Then she had demanded of my mother. *"Why is that child playing in your things?"*

My mother had raced across the room and grabbed me out of the chair, slamming the drawer closed. I'd been terrified. She'd set me outside the room and closed the door. Grandmother had shook a long finger at me, telling me that the boogieman came and carried away little girls who didn't stay where they belonged. I remember running to my room and crumbling to the floor between the wall and my bed, clutching Boo. Why had I kept that memory hidden all these years? Were others hidden as well? I had always been afraid of my grandmother, but I had thought it was the trauma I'd felt when she'd taken Boo. If she had been the one who had been responsible for bringing me here, why had she seemed to dislike me so? Libby would be saying a big mystery that I must get to the bottom of. As I touch the writing desk, I wish I'd been closer to my mother, that she would have told me years ago about the bell. If she hadn't whispered those words on her deathbed, would I have ever tried to find out anything? "Silly," I whisper, as the rain pounds harder on the roof. "If there is a way to find out about who I really am, I have to find the links, if anyway at all, no matter what I uncover." I shake my head, thinking that maybe I'm out of reality already, talking to myself. I reach for the small ivory knob, with the painted rose petal on top, and pull. The drawer is locked. I rummage in the side drawers, nothing there. Should be some tools in the garage I could use to jimmy the lock. I go down the stairs to the garage and flip on the light. On the far wall hangs a pegboard with all kinds of hand tools, probably untouched since my father's death. I take down a Phillips and a Flathead. I guess whoever buys the house will get the tools, as well as the things in the attic.

I return to the attic and begin to try to open the drawer. I'm able to slide the screwdriver between the top of the drawer and the desktop. I pry with all my strength. The front of the drawer splinters; tiny pieces of wood fall onto the floor. I pull away the rest of the drawer front. I swallowed hard, my heart pounding. Am I inches from a clue that will lead me to my roots?

Chapter Three

I see an envelope, along with several pens and a writing pad. I pull on the bottom of the drawer, and it slides towards me. I grab the envelope; an object slides out, tumbling back into the open drawer. My fingers tremble as I pick it up. Am I actually touching something that thirty years ago a person had touched for one last time, before placing it with a baby girl, then sending her on her way? I swallow a raw lump in my throat and concentrate on the object in my hand. It is in the shape of a half bell, with the zigzag cut right down the middle, just as Aunt Kate had said. I run my finger over the jagged edge. The object is made of wood about a half inch thick, a bright red color. A slender gold ribbon runs through a small round hole at the top. I pick up the envelope and peer inside. Empty. I shiver, realizing that the attic has gotten colder. Clutching the bit of wood to my chest, I turn off the light and go down the stairs.

In the kitchen, I sit on a barstool, lay the half bell on the counter top, and just stare. Did something so tiny hold a clue to who I really was? Had a loving mother, or perhaps a father, crafted this? But cutting it in two? That left me uneasy. Perhaps Aunt Kate was right; maybe I wouldn't like what I found, even if there was a way to find out where the bell came from.

God I need a cup of coffee. I leave the bell on the counter and prepare the coffee. For a few minutes, I watch the rain sliding down the windowpane. It looks so cold out there. I rub my hands up and down my arms, fingering the softness of my much-washed sweatshirt. I suddenly realize that everything I'd known since childhood would be gone in a few days. This house. Other people will come to live here. Did a house hold memories, embedded into its core forever? Had this house known happy times? Maybe when my parents had first moved here? Had they been in love, dreaming of a family of their own? Before I came? I don't like to think that my coming may have caused this house to turn cold. I turn on the oven and open the door; soon, the coil turns a bright orange, sending a welcoming warmth into the kitchen.

I take my coffee and return to the barstool. I pick up the bell and turn it over. There are tiny marks running across the backside. Pencil marks? I bring the bell closer. The markings are words. A clue? I squint, my heart racing. I can make out a word, then another: Bailey. Christmas 71.---The year I was born. I would have been three months old the Christmas of 71. A week before Christmas, was when I'd arrived here, my parents had told me. Another word? No. It's two words. Dell C O. Dell C O? A place? A company? C O? If it meant a state it would be Colorado. But what about the Dell? Was there a Dell Colorado? I'd certainly never heard of such a place. The Dell computer company? No way. I stare at the jagged bell, wondering where the other half was, if it even existed after all these years?

Maybe Aunt Kate knew more than she was telling. Maybe she would remember something about a Dell.---could be a person-- or maybe the family had known someone in Colorado some thirty years ago. Dreading, what I knew would be a lecture about letting the past lie, I reach over, take the kitchen phone off the wall and dial her number.

On the third ring, my aunt's voice tersely said, "Hello."

"Aunt Kate, this is Taylor," I said, surprised that my voice sounded strong, not shaky at all. I square my shoulders a bit, thrust out my chin, and say before she has a chance to speak. "Do you know if I have any connections to Colorado?"

A deep sigh from the other end of the line. "Taylor, are you really going ahead and digging into the past? I'd hoped you would take some good advice and just let it be."

"I found the bell, Aunt Kate!" I almost shout.

"Good Lord! It can only lead to trouble. Taylor why do you need to do this? Why can't you just let it be?"

"I need to know where I came from. Mother in the end understood that. And just maybe she had a sense of my needing to know in the future when she saved the bell from the fire. Why else would she have done it? And if finding out leads to disappointment, well, I can handle that. The bell has C O on the back. I think it might mean Colorado. Please, if you know anything tell me."

"Do you think you are actually going to find a new family, one who will welcome you with open arms? I think you are going to be headed for a fall, young lady."

"I'm not searching for a new family, Aunt Kate." I try to find the words to make her understand. "I just want to find out where I got my auburn hair, the freckles on my nose, where my interest in art came from."

"It shouldn't matter where you came from. It should only matter that my sister took you in and raised you as her own! You shouldn't pay her back by going off on some wild goose chase, looking up people who gave a child away. I'm not trying to sound harsh, Taylor, but those are the facts. Think about it. You owe your loyalty to your mother and father."

I realize it is useless to try to explain that this has nothing to do with loyalty to my parents. That it has nothing at all to do with them. And so, I ask again, "Can you think of any connection to Colorado? Do you think I could have been born there?"

"I haven't a clue as to where you were born. I know Caroline didn't know. Mother Winfield arranged it all. She worked it all through her lawyer,---and he's been dead for years, so don't go trying there. No one spoke of your adoption after she threw the records into the fire. *'This baby's past is forever dead,'* she said. And I for one think it was the right thing to do."

"But what right did she have to make a decision like that?"

"She ruled that household until she died."

From what memories I had of Grandmother Winfield, I didn't doubt what my aunt was saying.

"And you never heard Colorado mentioned at all?"

"Your Uncle David once told me that his mother spent a few months there, back in forty-nine or fifty. He thought she'd had a breakdown. That was while your grandfather was in Europe. There was a separation or something. The boys were only about four."

"Do you think there's a connection?"

"I don't see how. Think about it, Taylor. How in the world

could your grandmother spending a few months in Colorado some twenty years before you were even born possibly have anything to do with you? Use some common sense. Think about what you are doing. What are you going to do, look all over Colorado? You don't even have a name. What you are doing makes no sense at all."

I press on. "What about Dell? Could there be a place called Dell in Colorado? Or a Dell company, or person?"

"This is ridiculous, Taylor. Just give it up."

"I can't just *give* it up," I said.

"Well, I'm sorry for you," she said.

After we hang up, I get a notepad and pencil from the drawer and begin to write down what might be clues: Bell. Bailey. Colorado. Company. Dell. 1971 As an afterthought I scribble: Grandmother Winfield in Colorado 1949, 50.

By noon the rain had stopped, and the sun was playing hide and seek with a few stubborn, gray clouds. I'd called the storage company, and they will pick up my bedroom furniture tomorrow. Don't really know why I'm saving it. I have a storage bin full of furniture in Cincinnati. Perhaps it was needing to hang onto a little bit of growing up here. I really don't know. I just feel sad knowing that after Thursday, I'll never be able to just walk up to the door on this magnificent old home, turn my key in the lock and walk right in. It's like a part of me is being locked away. I might have not felt loved here, but I had been cared for, sheltered. Now, that, too, was gone. "Good, grief, Taylor," I say aloud, "One would think that you were an orphan, tossed into the sea of life without a lifeline." I shake my head at my wild thoughts, wondering if there's an age limit on being an orphan?

I wrap the bell in white tissue paper, I find on the shelf in the hall closet. My mother had always lined gift boxes with white tissue paper. The outside of presents she'd wrapped in fancy foil, then tied them up with elaborate ribbons and bows. I suddenly realized that this Christmas I wouldn't experience something that had been a part of me all my memories.

A sadness, a feeling of loss sweeps over me and tears

suddenly flood my eyes, spilling over to run down my face. I crumble to the floor, clutching the tissue-wrapped bell to my chest, and sob with total grief. Grief, I hadn't felt all those last days of my mother's illness, and I hadn't felt this loss even as we'd laid her to rest beside my father at Greenbrier Cemetery.

After a few minutes, my sobs cease, the tears stop, and I'm left feeling totally empty. Thursday. I'd have to be out of this house by Thursday. This house where my great-grandmother Millicent Cornell had come to as a young bride. She had been Grandmother Winfield's mother, had come here after marrying my great-grandfather, who had been a professor of literature at the local university.

Strangers will buy the house. Aunt Kate had said she wanted no part of it; that it would only remind her that her sister had been totally foolish and allowed a man to destroy the family name? Winfield. A proud old name. Taylor Winfield. What had my name been before it was Taylor Winfield? A proud name? A name shrouded in scandal? Would I ever know? But as I sat there on the cold tile floor of the house that I'd called home all my life and would have to leave forever by Thursday, I sat there and knew one true thing, that if there was anyway at all, I was going to find it.

Chapter Four

The next morning, Wednesday, the sun is streaming in my window, falling upon my face. I lie there for a few minutes and let my eyes take in the room: the cream colored wall paper, with a delicate rose pattern, so faint it's barely visible; the high oak wardrobe; matching chest of drawers, the bookcase with Bear, sitting just as he'd sat all those years ago, after I'd refused to let him replace Boo. I think I'd mourned Boo for most of my childhood, maybe a tiny bit of me still does. Silly thoughts, I tell myself and get out of bed. I walk to the window. Old man Hubbard is on his porch step, reaching for the newspaper. How many years had he done this each morning? How many times had the paperboy actually landed the paper on the porch? The old man leans on his walking cane and slowly makes his way up the step onto the porch. This is the first time I'd seen the cane. I blink back a tear. Everything is changing. And it seems that I, who was slow to tears since I'd sobbed my insides out over Boo all those many years ago, was finding tears coming easily. I don't like that. Don't need that.

I quickly shower, blow dry my hair and put it up in a ponytail, dress in jeans and a white sweatshirt with Mickey Mouse inscribed across the front in large satin letters of green, red, yellow and blue. I dig into the top drawer of the dresser and pull out a pair of yellow bobby socks. Most of my shoes were in that storage bin back in Cincinnati. I go to the closet and stare at what's left: A pair of brown loafers, black flats, a pair of black two inch heels, and a pair of Nike running shoes. I pick up the running shoes and put them on. The truck from the storage company is supposed to be here at nine. I strip off the bed linen and stuff it into the closet.

At precisely nine o'clock, a truck, with large printing on the side, announcing "Frank's Storage", pulls into the driveway.

By nine thirty, my bedroom furniture, along with the writing desk from the attic, is in the truck heading out of the driveway.

I get the bell and stand looking out the kitchen window. Dell

C O. Bailey. I run my finger over the words. These have to be clues; they just have to be. I grab my purse and car keys off the counter, go to the hall closet, take my navy, ankle-length, wool coat off a hanger, put it on and step into the December sunshine. I shiver as the cool air hits my face. It hadn't looked cold from the window. My windshield is frosted over. I start the car, then dig under the seat for the scraper. Soon, I've scraped off enough frost to let me see, and the heater has started to give just a little warmth. I back up, realizing that the rear window is still frosted. I trust to memory that nothing is in the drive behind me, back up, and then put the car into drive. The library should be open by now.

The library is an old brownstone building, two stories, built in 1920. My great-grandfather was instrumental in getting it built and has a wing with a donation of his personal library. How many hours had I spent here as a child? Mother had seen to it that I had books. She'd loved them as well, spending hours in her bedroom reading. She seldom read to me, nor did my father. They'd give me a book and say, *"Isn't this a nice book? You will love this one."*

After I'd learned what was between the pretty covers, I'd kept one close at hand. Growing up, I'd loved books about horses; my tears had dampened my copy of Black Beauty.

Inside, I approach the counter. A young, dark haired woman smiles at me. I tell her I'd like to use a computer, connected to the Internet.

"You're in luck," she said. "No one is signed up yet. You can stay on an hour, and if no one else wants a turn, you may stay another hour." She points to her left, towards a door marked "Computer Room".

Inside the room, I find three computers and sit down at the one in a far corner. I'm glad the room is empty. I'm soon on the Internet, and the Yahoo search engine appears on the screen. I take the bell from my purse, laying it on the table beside the computer. Dell Co. I type in the search line. About a thousand references to the Dell Computer Company. I zap that and type in Dell Colorado. One reference. I suck in my breath and click on the web page.

The site boasts: Home of Beautiful Dell Colorado. Gorgeous

scenery. Hot vacation spot for tourist from all over the world. Most delicious dining in all of Colorado, and the best lodging. The next line causes my heart to jump: And a multitude of craft shops, where award winning artists sell their creations. The Christmas crafts are already stocked.

I leave the Dell site, go back to the search engine and find maps. I type in destination Dell Colorado. Leaving from Scalesville, Indiana. I print out the map and turn off the computer. Over twelve hundred miles. Twenty-three hours to get there, the printout said. I put the map, along side the bell, into my purse and leave the library, wondering just what I'd find in Dell Colorado.

The next Morning, I awake before dawn and get out of the sleeping bag I'd found in the garage. The room is chilly. I pull on my fluffy pink terrycloth robe and go down the stairs. December the 14. Thursday. The last day this house will belong to someone named Winfield. I start a pot of coffee and listen to the silence of the house. It seems so quiet, so cold, so dead.

I take a cup of coffee to the back deck. A slow, cold wind sends shivers through me. I wrap my hands around the cup for warmth and sink deeper into my robe. I lean on the deck railing and look across the large back lot. This house sits on two acres, containing trees and flower gardens. My mother had loved tending her gardens. Would the new owner keep all the rose bushes?

The gray in the east is slowly becoming lighter, turning to soft shades of purple and pink. The last sunrise I'll see from this house. Who will come after me? Will a tiny bit of who we were linger here, long after the name of Winfield is no longer remembered?

A ray of sunlight streams from beneath a cloud, turning it to ribbons of gold. The sight is so beautiful, yet a wave of deep sadness sweeps across me, threatening to bring tears to my eyes. I swallow hard and go back inside.

By nine, I'm ready to go, to say good-by to this house. I put my luggage in the car and go back inside for one last time. From the top shelf of the hall closet, I take the photo album that holds snapshots and school pictures of my growing up days. I look inside my purse. The bell is secure inside the tissue wrapping. What will the next weeks reveal to me? Sure there's a good chance that in the end I'll find nothing at all. But one thing for sure, I will give it a try. Should I tell anyone that I'm heading for Colorado? If I should come up missing, who would know that I was even gone? The school, when I didn't show up for the new semester? I pick up the phone and dial Libby's number.

"Oh, Taylor," I was going to call you yesterday, but the lines were down, just got service back late last night. We had an ice storm. The power was out too. It was cold, good thing we have the two fireplaces and plenty of wood." Before I can say anything, she continues, "I'm just dying to hear about the bell. You did find it, didn't you?"

"I found it."

"Wonderful!" she almost screams. I hold the phone away from my ear.

"Tell all! Did you find out who your birth parents are? Did your mother leave you a letter, telling you why she had to give you up, and a way to find her if you ever wanted to? This is so exciting I can hardly stand it!"

"There was only the bell, with just a few words written on the back."

"What's written!"

"Dell, C O, Bailey, Christmas, 1971."

"Have you figured out what it all means? The 1971, of course, is the year you were born! Oh, Taylor, I'm so excited, I have chill bumps all over my arms!"

"I think the Dell C O may mean Dell Colorado."

"Bailey! Could be your name, either first or last. Well! What are you going to do? You are going to Dell Colorado? Aren't you? Of course you are. How could you not? Wish I could go with you. What an adventure!"

"I'm going, Libby." I tell her. "Just thought you should know." I don't tell her that I wanted someone to know where I've gone in case I'm never heard of again.

"You will find your roots. I just know it. You have to keep

me posted."

"I've got to go. I need to turn in the house keys to the bank by noon. You take care, and hug the boys for me. Love you."

"You be careful and I'll be thinking good, happy thoughts of you."

I hang up the phone, wishing I were as sure as Libby was that all would go well. I hoped my friend would always live in her fairytale heaven, with everyday filled with sunlight. She had willed her life to be just as it is. What would she do if suddenly all that came tumbling down? I hope she never has to find out.

By noon, I've gassed up the car, dropped the keys off at the bank and am turning onto I-70. I pat my cell phone on the seat beside me. I seldom used it, but it gave me comfort to have it, just in case. The early morning promise of sunshine had dwindled, and now large raindrops are splattering my windshield. I turn on the wipers. Hope it doesn't get cold enough to snow or worse, freezing rain.

The miles swirl by, sometimes in heavy rain, sometimes just a mist; once I ran through a patch of total sunshine. And a little farther on, rain started again, although the sun was still shining. A rainbow so beautiful, I pulled over to the side of the interstate and just stared. In fact, on looking closer, I saw that another one was shadowing the first. Libby would have seen it as a sign of good fortune for sure. I stood in the cool mist, on that highway just inside the Missouri border and hoped that the end of my journey would at least yield me answers. Answers to questions I'd had since forever. I had never felt so alone.

Chapter Five

Darkness had long since claimed the day, when I pulled into a Holiday Inn just outside Billington, Missouri. A sign, under the one welcoming everyone to Billington, boasted that it was a great place to visit, a better place to live. Population 35,032.

I checked in, then had a late supper at Rosie's, a little cafe just around the corner. Tina, the friendly, plump waitress told me I looked like a weary traveler. When I got back to my room and surveyed myself in the mirror, I agreed.

I took a quick shower and lay on the comfortable bed in the darkness. "Taylor Winfield, do you know what you are doing?" I whispered to the shadows.

I suddenly think of Alex. I hope he's happy in Seattle, this man I'd once thought would be my life's companion, my husband, the father of my children. He was, after all, what Libby would call a Prince Charming: Tall, handsome, with a smile that made you feel that you were all he saw. I'd thought I'd been totally in love, and I think he had thought he was as well. When after a few months, the glow of whatever it was we had faded, we both realized that there was nothing there. But by then we had moved to Cincinnati, each of us taking teaching jobs. Me as an art instructor, he as an assistant coach. He met Anne, the girls' athletic director in the same school. He'd felt guilty. I felt like a giant weight had been lifted off my shoulders. Love at first sight? How many couples have gone ahead and married, to later find that it was all surface, and beneath the thin layer they were calling love, was really nothing at all? Maybe a few like Alex and me would still think they had a friendship. He and Anne moved to Seattle, and I stayed in Cincinnati, until I got the phone call from Aunt Kate telling me that my mother's cancer was in its final stages.

I'd taken the leave from my job and rushed home. Marcus had been gone for months. I'd not liked him the first time I'd met him, and in those two years it had taken him to destroy my mother,

I'd probably seen him a total of three times. People live and people die and some leave destruction along the path they trod; others manage to leave a ray of sunshine, a ray of hope. I think I read that somewhere in one of the hundreds of books my mind had consumed over the years. I drift into sleep, wondering if I'll leave any path at all?

The next morning as I sip coffee made from the packets I'd placed in the two-cup coffeepot, I pull back the heavy drapes and am happy to be greeted by rays of sunlight. A good sign, Libby would say. This morning I like to think she's right.

I check out of the motel and walk around the corner to Rosie's cafe and have a quick breakfast.

By eight-thirty I'm back on I-70, and Billington, Missouri has already vanished from my rearview mirror. I was still about eight hundred miles from Dell. I'll stop again tonight, then have a better plan on where to go from there.

The sun shined on me all the way to Carryville Kansas. I found a motel and had dinner at a MacDonald's across the street, and then fell into bed by the time "Who Wants To Be A Millionaire" came on. I don't remember if anyone won. I awoke at five and was on the road by six.

The sun was sinking behind ribbons of gold and peach, when I pulled off the interstate to a sign that announced, with a pointed arrow: Dell exit. I'm soon off the exit ramp and traveling down a street called Morrison. Old-fashioned type lampposts with soft amber globes line each side of the street, with the posts wrapped in green garland tied off with huge red bows. I follow the street around a curve and turn onto a square, surrounding a small courthouse with a clock tower. The brick courthouse sits on a spacious lawn dotted with various sizes of evergreens, each adorned with hundreds, maybe thousands of white, miniature, sparkling lights. I drive around the courthouse, slowly, following a line of cars. The four blocks surrounding the courthouse contains buildings, store fronts, mostly two story, a bank, one newspaper office, the printing on the window in white says it is home of The Dell Tribune. The sidewalk is filled with bustling people.

I pull into a parking space. "Silver Bells" is playing faintly from the shop in front of me. "Edna's Fine Chocolates". For a few minutes, I just sit and stare at the people walking by. Old couples arm in arm. A family of four. A young couple pushing a stroller. Two teenage girls, sporting jackets in school colors of blue and white, on the back "Dell Tigers". One whispers in the other's ear, they giggle and head inside the candy store. It all looks so much like a Courier and Ives painting. God, it's all so beautiful. All that's lacking is snow. Could my roots really be here?

I back out of the parking space. I'd better find a place to stay. There'd been a Holiday Inn just off the exit ramp. I circle around the courthouse; the hands on the tower clock point to seven. I go back up the street I'd come down on. Before long, I'm pulling into the Holiday Inn. When I get inside and walk up to the desk, the desk clerk, an older man with snow-white hair, tells a young couple, "Well, Mr. and Mrs. Smith you just got our last room."

Not words I wanted to hear at all. I rest my hands on the counter. The clerk smiles at me. Mr. and Mrs. Smith look at me apologetically. Mr. Smith picks up the door card, puts an arm around a well-curved, blonde Mrs. Smith, and they go out the door.

"If you are looking for a room, miss, I'm sorry but we're all filled up. But, I'll be happy to call around and see if any of the others have anything left. With it being a Friday, we're getting busy, with the Christmas season coming on and all."

"I'd appreciate it if you'd make the call."

"Sorry, miss," he says after making three calls. "Everything is filled. It's like this every year at the Christmas Season. Where're you heading? You might find something at Morrisville about a hundred miles north."

I shake my head. "This is my stop."

A skinny, dark headed woman in a green uniform, holding a feather duster, comes out of the office area. "You should try Hattie's Bed and Breakfast. She might have something. She's been working on getting her place open."

"Thank you," I tell her. She smiles and nods and begins dusting a beautiful green plant. "Is her name in the phonebook?

Could I call?" I ask, turning back to the clerk.

"Tell you what, I'll call her for you, if you want."

"Please," I said.

"Her number is 555-3333," the maid volunteers, nodding at me. "Hattie is a friend of mine. She's going to have a really nice place. I'd not be allowed to steer you over there, if we weren't filled up here."

"It is very kind of you."

Meanwhile, the clerk has dialed. "This is Oliver, over at Holiday Inn. You got your place open yet? We're all filled up and we got a young lady here," he pauses, puts his hand over the receiver and turns to me. "You alone, miss?"

"I'm alone."

He takes his hand off the receiver, "She's alone." He hangs up the phone and smiles at me. "She's got one room that she'll rent out."

"You are very kind. And you, too, I tell the maid."

"Are you staying long?"

"Maybe a few days. I don't know yet."

"You'll find that Dell is filled with lots of good people," he said proudly. "To get to the Bed and Breakfast, you just stay on the street out there until you come to the first stoplight, turn left. Hattie's place is a big, old, white house, three stories, sits back a ways from the street. About two, three blocks down on the right."

I thank the two again and step into the cold December night.

Following the directions the clerk had told me, I'm soon at the stoplight. I turn left and look for a giant house on the right. Most of the houses are big. I've never stayed at a Bed and Breakfast. But I'm looking forward to a bath and a warm bed. What would I have done if the kind maid and clerk hadn't helped me find the Bed and Breakfast? Slept in the car? Was I really doing this? Being impulsive wasn't something I did. I'd never been impulsive, really. But I'd never gone off searching to how I was connected to a jagged, wooden half bell before either. I can almost hear Libby's voice, "You're on a grand adventure, Taylor! Listen to the little voice inside your head."

I spot a large Victorian house, a three-story with a balcony over the front wraparound porch, green garland with white miniature lights, tied off with giant red bows, snake massive white columns. "This is it. This has to be the place, please let it be the place," I whisper, turning onto a winding drive.

I shut off the motor and lights and just stare at the picture before me---another Courier and Ives. Would the room be available for more than tonight? Dummy, you haven't even seen the inside yet. What if the room isn't any good? And worse yet what if this Hattie person is a witch? What if the price for one night is outrageous? You can stand it for one night, you can afford it for one night--after all you have Master Card and Visa, worry about the cost after Christmas, when you get back to work, I tell myself and get out of the car. I unlock the trunk and take out my overnight bag and hesitate. Suppose this isn't the place, you'll look stupid standing on someone's porch with an overnight bag if it isn't. Still I go on.

From the porch I can see through the front window, another Courier and Ives setting. A tall Christmas tree, boasting many tiny lights of red, green and white, almost touches a high ceiling. A fire licks orange tongues at a log in the huge stone fireplace, where a tan and white collie stretches on a rug, along side a black and white cat. Friends? Of course. Two striped overstuffed couches, along with several chairs and a few tables and lamps makes me think of a picture on a Christmas Card. I ring the doorbell and am soon face to face with a smiling gray haired woman, who is wiping her hands on a white bib apron that says in large green and red lettering, "Merry Christmas".

She pushes the storm door open. "You are the stranded traveler they called about from the Holiday Inn. Come in, dear. Come on in here out of the cold. I'm Hattie. Hattie Conroy."

Breathing a sigh of relief, I step into a foyer. In one corner stands a Christmas tree, miniature of the one I'd seen through the window. A desk is to the right with a bell on top, along with several pens and a sign-in book, sitting beside a phone, answering machine combination. To the left is a stairway leading to the upper floor.

The railing is adorned with green garland and red velvet bows. By now the Collie has come to investigate and is licking my cold hand in welcome, viciously wagging a bushy tail. The cat seems to like me as well and rubs its face against my leg.

"Get away! Scottie," The woman said, swinging a hand at the dog. "And you, Jude, get back in the other room," she said, gently tapping the cat with a slippered foot.

The dog and cat trot into the adjoining room and flop on the rug before the fire.

"Hope you like dogs and cats," the woman said laughing, a laugh that I'd call absolutely happy. She walks behind the desk and turns the register book to face me, handing me a pen. "Those two," she said, waving a plump hand in the direction of the next room, "are what I call my troubleshooters."

Noting the puzzled look on my face, she continues, "They can tell better than me what kind of guest I'm getting. If a guest doesn't pass their test, I sleep with one eye open."

I can't suppress a laugh. "How did I do?" I ask, signing my name.

"I'll sleep sound tonight," she giggles.

There's a place for my address and phone number. Realizing that for the first time in my memory I have neither, I feel a wave of sadness sweep across me.

"Are you all right, dear?" The woman asks, touching my arm.

I look up, into a face filled with genuine concern. And without really thinking about it, I blurt out the truth. "I don't have an address or phone number at the moment, just my cell phone number. I'm between things, but don't worry, I can pay for the room," I said, taking my Master Card from my purse."

"Do I look worried?" she said, waving the card away. "We'll take care of the bill when you check out. She turns the register book around and looks at the name I'd signed. "Come on, Taylor Winfield. I'll show you to your room. You are the first one to sign this new register. I'm really not open yet. I'm redoing the whole upstairs and have only the one room done. Got old friends from Iowa coming in tomorrow. Hadn't planned on opening it up till after the first of the year, but they called yesterday, then I got the call from Oliver over at Holiday Inn and said what the heck." She leads the way to the stairs. I pick up my overnight case and follow.

"I have four guestrooms up here," she said, pausing on the landing, looking back over her shoulder. She goes down the hall, stopping at a door at the end of the hallway. "This is the best room," she said, opening the door, "and the only one finished. From this room you get a view of both the front and back yards. All the rooms have a private bath."

She flips on the light switch, revealing a large room with a comfortable looking, four-poster double bed. "Make yourself to home," She said, placing her hand on the doorknob. "And when you've gotten settled, come on down, and I'll fix you something to eat. Supper was hours ago, but I've got plenty of leftovers. You are hungry?"

"Yes. Yes I am," I answer, realizing that all I'd eaten had been a snack at noon when I'd filled up with gas. "But you don't have to go to any trouble. I can go back out, pick up something at a drive-through."

"Won't hear of it. I'll have you some hot chocolate." She goes through the door, closing it behind her.

I let my coat fall off my arms, go to the bed and just let myself fall backwards onto the white chenille spread. I spread my arms out and close my eyes. Exhausted, I lay there for a few minutes. My stomach growls, reminding me of Hattie's promise of food and hot chocolate. I get up and go into the small, but lovely decorated bathroom and splash water on my face, then dry off with a fluffy, pink and white striped hand towel. I stared at my reflection in the mirror above the sink. I don't look so good. If Scottie and Jude hadn't seen beyond my outward appearance, I doubt that Hattie would have seen me as a suitable guest. I take a pick from my purse and fluff up my bangs, then touch up my lips with cherry lip-gloss. Knowing that I'm looking the best I can at the moment, I go down the stairs.

Hattie is at the desk and looks up and smiles. "How was the

room and all?"

"Perfect," I tell her.

She comes from behind the desk. "Come on back. I have your supper all ready and waiting."

I follow her through a large dining room, with a mahogany table with ten chair pushed around. A centerpiece of garland and red candles sits in the center. We go through swinging French doors, into a large kitchen that looks like a splash of sunshine. The walls are a bright yellow; copper-bottomed pots and pans hang from a suspended pot rack over an island that has a sink and counter with a massive cutting board. Two shelves above the microwave hold about thirty cookbooks. The kitchen of a cook for sure. She waves me to a small table covered with a yellow and white checkered tablecloth, filled with a platter of cold cuts, several types of cheeses and fluffy, brown sandwich rolls. I take one of the two chairs pushed up to the table and sit.

Hattie brings two, thick, ceramic mugs to the table, then goes to the stove and removes a steaming sauce pan, brings it to the table and pours, then sets the pan on a yellow potholder. "Wait a minute," she said, going to a cabinet and pulling out a bag of marshmallows. She brings the bag to the table, sits and smiles at me. "Hot chocolate just isn't the same without a marshmallow," she said, plopping one into the cup sitting before her. "Have one," she offers.

I take one, slide it into my steaming cup and begin stirring with a spoon she offers. "Dig in," she said.

I pick up a roll, pour on mustard and pile on a slice of ham and cheddar cheese. "Um," I said, sinking my teeth into the best sandwich I've ever had.

"Made the rolls myself," Hattie said proudly, taking a sip of chocolate.

"This is so good. And you are so kind to offer me supper. I didn't think supper was the deal with a Bed and Breakfast."

"It's not. But I could tell you needed feeding. And I have plenty."

"I appreciate your kindness."

"It's nothing. Have you been to Dell before?"

"Not that I remember," I said. And then I find myself telling this woman, this stranger, who up until a few minutes ago I didn't know existed. I find that I'm unable to stop myself from telling her more about myself than I'd ever imagined telling a complete stranger. It's like a force inside me is spouting forth and I'm unable to stop the words. I tell her about growing up in Scalesville, about my parents, about Alex, about moving to Cincinnati, about my mother's deathbed revelation about the bell. It was as though I'd had to tell her. But this was a stranger. A total stranger. Maybe it was the hot chocolate that I'd so eagerly let warm up my insides, maybe it was the delicious food, maybe it was this Courier and Ives house, perhaps it was the outrageous sunny kitchen, and maybe it was this happy-faced woman who looked at me like she was my friend. Whatever it was, it was beyond my control.

"What a story, dear," Hattie said, reaching over and squeezing my hand. "I've always loved a great mystery. And you have one for sure. And to think the answer to it all could lie right here in our little town of Dell, Colorado. It's so exciting that I've got goose bumps on my arms."

Now she's sounding like Libby.

"I wish you could stay here all the time you're in Dell," she said thoughtfully, taking a slow sip of her chocolate. "But I already have my friends coming in from Iowa who will be here tomorrow night. And I'm betting with all the tourists in town this time of year that all the motels are already booked solid. But don't you worry, something will turn up, you just wait and see."

"I'll find something tomorrow."

"I hope you find what you are looking for, dear," Hattie said.

I look into her sharp blue eyes and think that I've found a friend. Although I don't understand what has just gone on here. Never in my life have I been so open with another. But telling Hattie everything had seemed so natural; it was as though we'd talked like this always.

Scottie, closely followed by Jude, comes into the room, goes to the back door and scratches. Hattie gets up and opens the door.

"Don't be long," she tells the dog and cat as they bolt out the door. "They are just like children," she laughs.

I stand and push my chair up to the table. "Thank you for dinner."

"I enjoyed the company and conversation. If you want anything, juice, food. Anything. You feel free to come down here and help yourself."

"Thank you. That's very thoughtful of you."

"It was nothing," Hattie says, smiling at me, then turning to a scratching sound at the door. She opens it and Scottie and Jude run through. Scottie licks her hand, as Jude twists himself around her leg. She squats down, puts one arm around the dog and picks up the cat in the other.

"I'm going to turn in now," I tell her, thinking what a warm feeling this sunny kitchen has.

"Sleep well," she said, looking at me over the dog and cat, whose heads are resting under her chin. "I start serving breakfast at six-thirty, and it is available until eight."

"Goodnight," I said, leaving her with her arms wrapped around the animals.

Inside the room, I turn on the light, then turn it off again and walk across the room to the door that opens onto a small balcony overlooking the back yard. I pull open the door and step into the cutting December air. I shiver and rub my arms. My teeth are chattering, still I stand there and look out across the yard below. At the end of the yard is a cottage shadowed by two tall evergreens. I wonder if it goes with this house? A light is on in the upstairs window. All this seems so surreal, the Christmas card like setting, Hattie, the dog and cat. Perhaps it is all a dream, and I will awaken in my apartment in Cincinnati, my mother will still be in the house in Scalesville, and the bell won't exist. Only the sting of the December wind, threatening to freeze me, tells me it is real. Suddenly a dark figure is silhouetted in the window of the cottage. A figure of a man. Is he staring at me? I go inside and close the door.

Later, snug in the soft bed, under a mound of quilts, I hear tiny pecking sounds against the window. Sleet. Would I awaken to an ice storm? As I snuggle deeper into the bed, I feel that it doesn't matter at all; for now I am safe and warm.

Chapter Six

I awaken to sounds in the hallway: Toenails scraping on hardwood, followed by "You two get down here! You know better than to go up there!"

I lay there in the shadows, wondering what time it is? What time had Hattie said breakfast was? I fumble for my watch on the nightstand, find it and push on the illumination button. It lights up to reveal the hands at six-thirty. I snuggle deeper under the covers, not wanting to leave this warm, cozy nest. Well, the choice is all mine, I think dreamily. I don't hear sleet pelting the windows. Did that mean a snow or sunshine, or a cloud filled day? Whatever kind of day lay ahead the most important thing would be to find a place to stay. That Iowa couple would be snuggled in this bed in another morning. Maybe the good Lord sent a foot of snow to block their way. I giggle at my silliness.

I doze off, to dream of a field-cut Christmas tree trimmed with silver garland and hundreds of gaily colored, handcrafted bells. And on one of the lowest branches, right near the front, hangs a half bell with zigzagged edges. I'm fully awake now, my body trembling. The room is bathed in gray light. I get out of bed and rush to the window. A dusting of white covers the floor of the balcony. Nothing to keep the Iowa couple from taking this room. I go to the bathroom and begin to prepare for the day. I dress in jeans and a yellow, turtleneck sweater. Viewing myself in the mirror I decide that I look ok.

I go downstairs. The rug in front of the fire in the large room is empty. Wonder if Hattie banished Scottie and Jude to the outside? In the kitchen, Hattie sits at the table, a cup in her hand. "Good morning," she said and started to rise.

"Please don't get up," I said, helping myself to a mug from a tree rack. "Mind if I sit here with you?"

"Glad to have your company, but I'm going to fix your breakfast." She starts to rise again.

"I'll just have coffee," I said, pulling out a chair and sitting down.

"Nonsense. I'll get your breakfast. Would you like to eat in here or at the dining room table?

"Here will be fine."

What would you like? I have ham and eggs and biscuits and gravy."

"I'm not a big breakfast eater. I'll just have some toast, and jam if you have it."

She laughs. "I have the best strawberry jam in Dell Colorado. Made it myself. Have my own strawberry patch, back of the guesthouse. Raise a lot of vegetables. This place sits on two acres."

"The cottage in back? Does that go with this place?"

"It does. Bradley West lives there. He's a writer. Doing some writing, as a matter of fact, about a woman here in Dell. Guess he's sleeping in, or he'd have been in here for breakfast."

A bell rings. "That'll probably be someone looking for a place to stay," she said, pushing back from the table. "I'll be right back and fix you that toast."

I sip my coffee and look about the sunny kitchen. How warm this whole house feels, almost like it wrapped one in a cozy blanket. I've never felt this way about a house before, not the big house I grew up in, not my apartment in Cincinnati, not the small one Alex and I shared at the university. I get out of my chair and go to the breadbox, which is adorned with a spray of white daisies with bright yellow centers. There is homemade bread inside, and I put a slice into the nearby toaster. I felt comfortable helping myself. I look out the window, past cheerful yellow curtains. The sun is trying to push away low, gray clouds. At the end of the massive yards sits the two-story cottage. It looks like a gingerbread dollhouse.

By the time Hattie returns, I'm sitting at the table eating the toast, smothered in strawberry jam I'd found on a lazy Susan sitting on the counter. "Now, dear," Hattie said, hurrying into the kitchen, "what can I fix you? You need more than toast."

"I've had plenty. I really have to get out of here and look for a place to stay,"

"There's nothing available in all of Dell. The couple out

there said they had looked all over Dell and had called hotels in the closest two towns. I hate for you to go all the way to Monroe or Kylesboro," she said, looking at me like she'd worry. "Good luck on finding out about your roots and who made the bell. And give me a call, let me know how things turn out even if you don't get back here."

"I'll do that," I tell her.

"I do wish you could stay here," she said, just as the phone rang. She goes to the foyer to answer. A moment later she's back, grinning broadly. "My friends from Iowa cancelled out."

I can hardly belief my luck. "I get the room?"

"You got it."

"I'll unpack the rest of my things before I go into town."

"You'll want to park in the parking area to the side of the house since you're staying," Hattie said. "I wouldn't try to go into town in your car; it'll be bumper to bumper. You'd be better off walking; it's only six blocks."

I pull my car to the parking area to the side of the house, get my suitcases out of the trunk and head back inside. Now, I won't have to spend precious time driving miles and miles. Time to search. I go back upstairs and put my luggage inside the room, take the bell from my purse and stand by the window clasping it to my chest as I look down on Hattie's lawn. The dusting of snow is melting a bit, revealing brown grass. One week until Christmas. One week to find out if my bell had its roots in Dell Colorado.

I hold the bell to my face and close my eyes, trying to imagine the person who had crafted it. Why had she cut it in two? Did she have auburn hair? Were her eyes green? What if I never find the answers? That thought left me sad. Was I forever to have this void, like a hole in my heart? A hole I'd had since I'd been eight years old. I suddenly realize that the hole had been there long before then. I let my thoughts drift back in time, trying to recapture that first time I'd felt the hole. Was it when Grandmother Winfield took Boo away? No, it was before that. I don't think there was actually a first time for the hole, I think it was with me always. Had the person who had fashioned this bell, then cut it in half, felt a hole in her heart as well? Why did I always imagine the person crafting the bell as a her? What were the possibilities that a young man, my father, had made the bell, sending half with a daughter he was giving away? Maybe. I sigh and put on my coat, tucking the bell into its deep pockets.

Outside, I begin walking towards town, digging my hands into my pockets, my right one wrapping around the bell. The air is crisp, and clouds are at times blocking the sun. Perhaps before the day was gone, snow would be falling. I'd like that. I walk briskly and in a few minutes reach the business section. The sidewalks are jammed with people, and cars are bumper to bumper all along the streets.

I'm shoulder to shoulder with all sizes and shapes of people. I push my way through the crowd into a packed shop. The sign above the doorway says "Polly's Little Ole Candle Shop." Two smiling cashiers are busy behind a counter, scanning item after item as dozens of people, carrying all types and colors of candles, inch their way along the counter. I find an empty spot in a back corner and look around. Towards the back, a green tree decorated with tiny candles of green and red, reaches to the ceiling. Nothing but candles in here. The only other decoration is a giant Santa that winks and waves his hand. I look again at the busy cashiers and line of customers and decide that I'll not get into the line, maybe come back when it isn't so busy and show the bell. I shoulder my way out of the shop and slip into the crowd of noisy people; most are smiling, and they actually don't seem in a hurry at all. I suddenly realized that it was I who had been rushing through the mass of people, and everyone else, except for maybe a frustrated kid or two, were just ambling along. Did things really move slower in places like this?

I stop before a window with a small green tree inside. My heart skips a beat; the tree is decorated with all kinds of wooden ornaments: Tiny soldiers, balls of many colors, silver stars, little teddy bears, and tiny presents tied with bows, but not one bell. Doesn't mean the person making all these ornaments never crafted a bell, I tell myself and push open the door. Tacked to the tops of the door, tiny green and brown jingle bells, on a black leather strap, gently announce my entrance.

Several customers are milling around in the small shop. One lady, dressed in an expensive looking, tan, ankle-length wool coat which cover the tops of shiny brown leather boots, flips her shoulder length dark hair and looks up at her companion. "Just look at these, Peter," she said, holding up several wooden soldiers. "Aren't these marvelous? Now, I know exactly how I will decorate the tree in Jonathon's room. He'll love these little guys. And I will add all wooden ornaments. Won't that be charming?"

"Wonderful," the man replies, looking at the beautiful woman as if anything she said would be just *wonderful*.

I wrap my hand around the half ornament in my pocket, wondering what the stunning woman's reaction would be to a wooden ornament that was only half there. Would she think it extraordinary and want one for her own, or would she recoil in horror, wondering why anyone would produce just half of something?

I dig into the large bin filled with dozens of gaily-colored, wooden balls, each one with a tiny red or green bow attached through a perfectly round hole in a knob on its top. I select two, one red with silver stripes, the other green with gold stars. I get in line behind two other customers.

"Find everything you wanted?" Asked the cashier, a thin, smiling woman, with short, gray curly hair, who looked to be in her sixties.

"Yes. I'll take these," I said, handing her the ornaments. "Did you make these?"

"Heaven's no," she said laughing. "I could never make something so skillfully crafted. Sarah Fluty makes all our wooden ornaments; our best sellers, I might add. I tell her that I bet her work is in homes all across the country, and beyond. Last year, a lady from New Zealand was in here and bought a sack full of her stuff."

"Does the artist live in town?"

41

"Yes. I can't tell you just where though, don't think she'd appreciate that. No offence to you dear," she says, patting my hand gently. "But I don't want to be the source of droves of people showing up on her doorstep."

"I understand," I tell her.

"There was a story about Sarah in last Thursday's paper," the woman continues, "and a writer here in town is doing a book about crafters and Sarah is going to be in it."

I hand her the money for the balls and take my change. I'd like to ask more about this Sarah person, but realize that I'm taking up far too much time, by now a line of people are impatiently waiting. Guess it would be better to come back later and show her the bell.

"Have a wonderful day," she tells me, then turns to the next customer, "Find everything you need?"

I walk out of the store wondering how I was going to find Sarah Fluty?

Chapter Seven

I step onto the sidewalk in the midst of other shoppers. What a busy happy place. I round another corner and go inside a shop with a sign in the window proclaiming "You want it. We got it." A rack of handmade quilts lines a back wall. One whole side has shelf after shelf of beautiful dolls, each seeming so real, almost like they could speak, laugh, or cry. A long table holds lovely wreaths of fresh greenery, tied with scarlet bows, but no wooden ornaments.

I go to the counter and wait in line behind a woman buying two of the dolls. "These are so real looking," she said to the cashier. "I'm getting this one with the pouty face for my granddaughter who looks just like this every time she doesn't get her way. And the other one, with her thumb in her mouth, is for my sister. She always sucked her thumb when she was a kid; she'll love this."

"I sell so many of these dolls," the cashier said. "Made by Dell's very own Carmen Richards."

"What talent," the customer said in appreciation.

"Dell is full of talented people," the clerk smiles.

"I'm looking for wooden ornaments, bells in particular," I tell her, when she gets to me.

"We don't have that. Sorry. But if you go three block north, you'll find some in Barbara Benson's shop. She's the only one in town who's commissioned to sell Sarah Fluty's wooden ornaments. Sarah's work is really popular. I hear that next year she's going to be selling her ornaments over the Internet."

I'm surprised that this person would be singing the praises of items she doesn't carry herself, and instead of trying to sell me a wreath or something is telling me where I can find what I want, from a competitor. Like something out of Miracle on 34th Street. "Where would I find the newspaper office?" I ask, thinking that I'd see what the story on Sarah Fluty would tell me.

"When you get to Barbara's place," she said, pointing north. "You'll be right across from the courthouse. Go across the courthouse lawn, cross that street and you'll be right in front of the

Dell Tribune. But they are closed on Saturdays. If you want to place an ad or something, you'll have to wait til Monday."

"I just want to get a paper. Thursday's paper. I heard there's a story about the ornament lady in it."

"There was. And if you go into the cigar store right next to the Tribune, I'll almost guarantee you'll find a paper. Bob Freely sells the paper, and he always has back issues.

I didn't tell the lady that I'd already been in Barbara's shop and had two Sarah Fluty ornaments in my pocket. I step out onto the sidewalk. A single snowflake lands on my nose. I make my way back to Barbara's shop, then cross the street through bumper to bumper traffic. Everyone is jaywalking. And the people in the cars don't seem to mind and just inch on. I can see what Hattie meant by not driving.

I make my way on the sidewalk crisscrossing the courthouse lawn, resisting the urge to shortcut it through the brown grass. I stop in front of Bob's cigar store. In the window, a large wooden Indian holds a box of cigars. A bell jingles as I open the door and step into a smoke filled room. Several men in caps, drinking beers out of bottles, sitting at a long table in the back of the room look up in surprise. Most nod. A heavyset, balding man, looking to be in his sixties, comes across the room. "May I help you, young lady?"

"I'd like a copy of Thursday's Tribune."

He goes to the counter and hands me a paper.

I take the paper. "How much?" I ask rummaging in my purse for change.

He waves a hand, "No charge. It's an old paper," he said, grinning.

"Thanks," I said. I go out of the store and take a deep breath of fresh air.

I decide to go back to my room and read the paper. I stuff it into the pocket of my coat and begin walking. By the time I'm within sight of the bed and breakfast, snowflakes as big as quarters are slowly drifting to the ground. I stop and just stare at the picture before me. The evergreens, with the soft white lights, Hattie's large house with the greenery, with the lights running through, topped off with the red bows. The snow drifting slowing down. A Christmas card for sure.

Inside, Scottie wags a welcome, and Jude rubs his back against my leg. "Any luck?" Hattie asks, coming from the kitchen.

"I found some wooden ornaments, but not one bell."

"Got anymore of that coffee, Hattie?" A sleepy voice said as a tall man comes through the French doors, carrying a coffee mug. Suddenly I'm looking into bloodshot eyes, inside a face that is covered with at least a two-day old stubble. Good thing for him that Hattie knows him. Surely she'd never let something looking like that inside her house if she didn't.

Hattie takes his cup. "Bradley, this is Taylor Winfield," she said, pouring coffee into the mug. "And Taylor, this is Bradley West."

"Hi," he said, twisting his lips like he's trying hard to smile, but it only looks like a grimace. He takes the coffee mug from Hattie and tells her thanks, eyeing me over the rim as he takes a drink.

"Nice to meet you," I said. Why do people always say that, even if it's not anywhere near the truth? Before he can say that it was nice to meet me as well, and lie as much as me, I said to Hattie, "I didn't see a grocery store. Where is the closest? I'd like to get a few things."

"The Milk Barn is probably your best choice if you just want to grab a few items. It's straight through town, a few blocks out. We have a giant Super Mason, just south of town, about a mile or so."

I tell Hattie thanks and start out the room.

"Well, I guess I'd better get going," this Bradley person said. I turn around as I reach the French doors and look back. He's setting his coffee mug on the table and looking at Hattie. I feel a bit ignored that he didn't at least lie and tell me he was glad to make my acquaintance. Really, Taylor why in the world did it matter if a grungy, bloodshot-eyed-stranger noticed you?

"I wish you'd let me fix you something to eat," Hattie said.

"Thanks, Hattie, but I just need a few hours of sleep. Have a good day," he said, going toward the backdoor. I watch, and can't think of one good reason why, as he opens the back door and goes through, closing it behind him.

"Poor man," Hattie said. "He's so tired. He's a writer you know." She looks at me like she's waiting for me to say something

I just say, "See you later," and go through the doors.

In my room, I spread the newspaper on the bed. The room is spotless. Hattie had tidied up while I'd been in town.

Could the disheveled creature I'd seen downstairs have also written the article on Sarah Fluty, as well as doing a story about her in a book? I hastily flip through the paper and find the article. A full-page spread. Naw, that rumpled creature hadn't written it. Someone named Blake had the byline.

I go to the balcony door and look out. Snow flakes, although not as large as earlier, are falling harder and have totally covered a fenced in garden to the right side of the cottage. Two giant evergreens touch arms at the edge of the garden. A cardinal swoops out of the sky, landing on a partially covered branch of one of the evergreens. The red, white and green makes me wish I had my camera. Before I can decide if I have time to retrieve it from underneath my car seat, the bird flaps its wings and flies away, leaving a slightly shaken bough to deposit a salting of snow to the ground. I wish I had my painting supplies from the storage bin in Cincinnati. Silly wish. No time to paint. It's just that with all the lovely scenes in this place, it makes me feel the need to create on canvas the beauty my eyes see. I remind myself that I didn't come to this place to paint, no matter how beautiful the settings are. I'm here to find the origin of a jagged edged Christmas Bell.

My stomach rumbles, reminding me that I should get a few snacks when I make it to the Milk Barn or the Super grocery. I stare at the cottage across the way, wondering if Bradley West is sitting at a computer, or would someone like him write on an old typewriter?

I go back to the bed and stare at the open newspaper. Why am I hesitant to read about this Sarah Fluty person? She made Christmas ornaments. I'd seen that in town. I admit to myself that ever since I'd gotten the paper, I'd had the thought tucked somewhere deep in my mind. *What if this person turns out to be my birth mother?* What do I do then? Find her studio; say "Hey! Remember me? You threw me away thirty years ago." You are being irrational, I tell myself, knowing full well that I'd never do such a thing, even if she had just thrown me aside. Maybe there was a good reason to have given a child away. By the second paragraph, I know that whoever Sarah Fluty is, she hadn't given birth to me. The sentence read, This thirty-two year old works at home in a studio. Only two years older than me. I finished the article. She'd been born in nearby Berne, the daughter of Deborah and the late Stanley Fleeming. Married to Owen Fluty. When she's not working in her studio, she's hiking and skiing with Owen.

"What one would call a perfect life, I guess," I hear my own voice say, sounding strange and echoing in the silent room. The article goes on to say that Bradley West a freelance writer from Dell is working on a book and that Sarah will be featured in it.

My stomach rumbles again. I really should try to find a grocery, or get a bite somewhere, maybe find a MacDonald's or Taco Bell or something. I look out the front window. The branches on the evergreens on the front lawn are covered with snow. Suppose, I don't find out anything at all? Suppose, I'm on a wild goose chase? Suppose I go through life and never know who threw away a perfectly good baby girl? A sadness fills my heart. Why did it matter so much? Why couldn't I just do as Aunt Kate had said, just forget about it, just leave such a big, big part of me a mystery forever? Maybe that's the reason, perhaps this big, big part of me is lost out there somewhere, and I need to find it to put me all together. Something like a jigsaw puzzle. It's no good without all the pieces. So what if I don't find one piece to the puzzle here in Dell, Colorado? What happens next? Do I spend my entire life, searching, looking for something that may be hidden from me forever? I blink back a tear. I really have to stop this. I'd never considered myself to be one who would waste time in self-pity, surely I wasn't doing that. If I don't find my roots this Christmas season, would I look again? How much of my life would be spent searching for something that I might never find? I suddenly know the answer: Forever.

47

The snow is falling so hard now that I can barely see the streetlight on the corner.

Just then a knocking on the bedroom door. I walk across the room and open the door to find a smiling Hattie. "Wanted to invite you to supper," she said, wiping her hands on an apron that has a giant Christmas tree and the words "Happy Holidays". "I've cooked up a slue of stuff. I always get in a wild cooking mood this time of year," she laughs. "Please say you'll come."

"I'd love to. It's so kind of you to ask me."

"It'll be ready in about an hour."

"I'll be there."

After she leaves, I close the door, wondering if Bradley West will join us? I hope so. Maybe I'll show him my bell. He's writing about crafters, maybe he's seen something like it.

I take the bell from my coat pocket and sit in the overstuffed chair near the front window. I run my finger along the jagged edges, close my eyes and try to imagine what could have been the thoughts of someone who put this jagged half bell along side a baby they were giving away. If she'd cared, why hadn't she sent along a letter to be read when that baby was all grown up and searching, or maybe when she was twelve and wanting so desperately for someone to tell her that she was special, that she would grow out of being an awkward adolescent. And later when she was in her twenties that maybe Alex wasn't the one who she should go away with, to try to start a life, and that there was more, so much more. Perhaps tell her that love, like in Libby's forever after, happy fantasies, really did exist. Could the answer to some or all of that really lie in the origins of an old bell? Now, that would be a story for someone like Mr. Bradley West to write about. Why does that name, that face of the unshaven man play in my thoughts? I get up and dig through my suitcase. Maybe I can find something to wear to supper that isn't as rumpled as Bradley West's shirt.

Chapter Eight

By the time I've gotten a shower, dried my hair and touched it up here and there with the curling iron, and dabbed on a touch of makeup, it's almost six and I'm so hungry I could swear that my stomach is touching my backbone. I slip on a pair of jeans. My dress slacks are wrinkled. Maybe Hattie will loan me an iron if I need to dress up for something, don't know what, but.... I pull on my light blue rib-knit turtleneck. I pick up the bell, then lay it back on the nightstand, turn off the light and stand at the balcony window. A light is on in the upstairs window of the cottage, and a figure is walking back and forth in front of it. Is Bradley West creating in his head what he'll later put on paper?

Down stairs, Hattie greets me warmly. The apron is gone, and she is wearing a red pants suit. "Come on into the kitchen. I have to let Scottie and Jude out." I follow her through the dining room; the table has been set with white china, a green and red tablecloth and matching napkins. Hattie opens the backdoor, and immediately Scottie and Jude rush past me, bolting through the open door into the snow. Hattie laughs. "They will be back scratching at the door in no time."

The aroma of fresh baked bread tantalizes my nose, reminding me of the hunger that has been in my belly all afternoon.

"Hope you're hungry," Hattie said.

"Starving. The smells are wonderful," I said.

"Bradley will be joining us. I'm so looking forward to dining with you young people," Hattie grins broadly. "When I had a Bed and Breakfast, over on Harrison Street, many, many years ago it was, I used to pick one night a week when I'd have some of the guests to dinner. I love good conversation. Keeps an old mind from going stale."

"Go on into the dining room and sit, dear," Hattie said. "Bradley will be here shortly, and I'll bring in the food. We'll just eat family style tonight."

"Can I help you with anything?" I ask, touched by her going to all this trouble.

"You just sit down," Hattie said.

I go into the dining room and sit in a high-backed chair. Soon, Hattie comes in, carrying a platter of golden fried chicken, then darts back and brings out a huge tray filled with bowls of vegetables and a gravy boat. She goes back again, emerging with a basket of rolls.

Hattie surveyed the table and smiled, pleased. Just then a scratching and a knocking at the backdoor. "Told you those two wouldn't be long. And that would be Bradley, also."

Scottie and Jude are soon in the dining room sniffing. "You two get in the living room and take a nap on your rug," she said, shooing them through the French doors.

"I'm starved, Hattie....," Bradley West said, coming through the door, stopping and looking at me in surprise .

"Sit down, Bradley," Hattie said, motioning to the chair directly across from me. "I'm so glad you young people are joining me tonight," she said, sitting in the chair at the end of the table.

I can't help noticing that Bradley West cleans up rather well. Hattie begins passing the food, and I as well as Mr. West dig in hungrily.

"Hattie you are the best cook in Colorado," Bradley West said, taking another helping of peas. "So, Miss Winfield, how are you enjoying your visit here in Colorado? Will you be here through Christmas?"

"Most likely, and it's absolutely lovely," I said. "The whole town reminds me of a Courier and Ives painting."

"Why, Bradley was saying the very same thing," Hattie said, smiling, looking at him, then back at me. "Just this afternoon we were looking out the front window at the snow falling on the evergreens, and you said," she leans to her left a little, laying a plump hand on his arm, "You said it's all so beautiful, just like a Courier and Ives painting."

I can't help noticing how really handsome he is. A wisp of dark hair falls over his forehead.   He looks at me and smiles. I smile lightly and look away. I'd felt something; a shiver, or maybe one would call it a tingle, going from the back of my neck clear down to my toes.

Hattie is looking pleased as she dips herself a large dollop of mashed potatoes and says, "Save room for a piece of my special cheesecake?"

"Did you get much writing done?" Hattie asks, looking at Bradley.

"Not much."

"You'll get it written before the deadline. You always do."

"Sometimes, I wonder if I'll make it." Bradley said.

"You've never missed one yet, have you?"

"Not yet," Bradley said.

As we eat, I learn that Bradley West was born just outside Denver, worked in New York as a magazine editor, then one winter started home to Denver for a visit, stopped off in Dell for the night; loved it so much that he found Hattie's cottage for rent and decided that he'd just stay here and write.

"Now, about you, Miss Winfield? Tell us something about yourself."

"I teach art at a junior high school in Cincinnati."

"Lots of artists paint what they see in this scenic place. Did you come to Dell to do some painting?"

"No. Actually I'm looking for the origin of a handmade ornament, a Christmas bell. By the way, I read an article in the Tribune about a local artist who does handcrafted ornaments; it mentioned about you writing the book, Crafters, in which she is featured."

"Yes. Sarah Fluty. She might know about the type of bell you have and if it originated in these parts."

"That would be a lead," I said.

"Give her a call. She's in the book. But she's out of town right now. Should be back in a couple of days. I'm sure she'd be glad to help if she can."

"Thanks." I turn to Hattie, "The dinner was delicious, thank you so much for having me."

51

"It was my pleasure, having both of you here tonight. How would you young folks like to take cheesecake and coffee by the fire in the living room?"

Remembering the effect Bradley West had had on me, I knew I'd be awkward alone with him. I suddenly feel a wave of resentment that this man, this stranger, could cause me to feel awkward. Maybe I should just go back to my room. How dare you, a voice deep in my head seems to shout. How dare you allow anyone, no matter how piercing brown his eyes are to have this effect on you.

"That would be lovely," I hear myself saying, "but I insist on helping clean up. That way all of us can enjoy your coffee and cake."

It wouldn't hurt Mr. Bradley West to lend a hand as well, I'm thinking, and look up to see him pick up his dishes and head towards the kitchen.

"You are my guests," Hattie protests, but I feel she's pleased that we are helping.

I stack an empty bowl onto my plate, put my ice tea glass in along with my silverware and follow Hattie, who is carrying the rest of the dishes into the kitchen. Bradley is standing at the sink, rinsing his plate, with a yellow and white checkered dishtowel thrown over his shoulder, like he's used to this. Maybe he's married? And for some reason that matters, that matters a lot. But he didn't have a ring, did he? Surely I would have noticed. I set my dishes on the counter and find myself looking over at his hands. No ring. But that didn't necessarily mean that he wasn't married, did it? I really should go back to my room and get a good night's sleep. I'll be myself in the morning.

"Bradley is writing a novel," Hattie said, looking at me, then back at him.

"That's interesting," I said, looking at him, realizing that I really was interested.

"How's it going with the publisher? Hattie asks, taking a plate out of his hand, putting it into the dishwasher. "The last time we talked about it, you were telling me they wanted you to change it."

"It didn't work out with that publisher," he said, shaking his head, squinting his eyebrows together. I sense a bit of anger here. "They wanted so many changes that my character became a totally different person. No sense writing in the first place if you let someone do that to your character," he said with so much passion in his voice that I got the tingle again."

"So, what did you do?" I asked.

"I'm trying to find another publisher."

"You stick to your guns," Hattie said, patting him on the shoulder. "He let me read part of it," she said. "It's wonderful. That publisher doesn't know from nothing. Readers know. And I'm a reader. From the time I was a little girl, I've loved books. I love the ones that grab a hold of me and won't let go until I've read the last word. Bradley's book is like that. I want him to hurry and finish it, so I can know what happened. I remember," she pauses, laughing, "when I was just about halfway through the chapters he'd given me. I had read until midnight, then tore myself away, telling myself that I just had to get to sleep. Well, I dozed off and was wide-awake two hours later with those chapters in my hand."

As I look at Hattie, see the excitement in her eyes, I find myself wishing I could get my hands on Bradley's book.

"Hattie's passionate about books," Bradley said, handing her the last dish.

"You wait," Hattie said, bobbing her head up and down. "A publisher with some sense will read your book and then all readers will have an opportunity to experience what I did."

"What is your novel about?" I ask.

"It's based on an incident that happened right here in Dell at the turn of the century."

"I remember my grandmother talking about the incident," Hattie said, nodding her head at me. "And to think that Bradley could take it and turn it and the characters into something so riveting. You see, Taylor, a young woman disappeared and was never found. A man who was a recluse was accused of murdering her. Nothing was ever proven, but two families were ruined. What

Bradley did with that story is amazing."

"You found out what really happened?"

"No. I just had some theories. Once I got to writing, it was as if the characters told the story themselves. I changed the names of course."

"Isn't that amazing?" Hattie asked.

"It is," I said. I remember reading about an author who said that all they did when they wrote was hold the pen. I look at Bradley West, wondering if he's that kind of writer?

"You two go on into the living room and make yourself comfortable. I'll put on fresh coffee. Maybe by the time it's ready, you'll like cake as well."

"Shall we?" Bradley said, smiling. I step ahead of him. I stop at the door to the room with the giant Christmas tree. A lamp and the fire's dying embers give a soft glow to the room. I hear hurried scraping sounds on the hardwood floor of the foyer; suddenly Scottie darts around us with Jude at his heel. They flop on the rug before the fireplace.

Bradley walks to the fireplace, pulls back the brass and black fire screen, kneels on one knee and lays a couple of small logs on the fire. Soon tiny flames are licking at the logs. In another minute the flames leap higher, sending more light into the room. As I watch the firelight flickering on his handsome face, I think that he is at home here in Hattie's place.

I stand at the window and stare out at the snow covered lawn, betting that at least another inch had fallen since I'd arrived for dinner.

"Looks just the way Christmastime should," Bradley West said, standing so close I can smell his aftershave. Old Spice. That tingle again. Could it be a warning? I move an inch or two away. Libby and I had decided, when we were fourteen, that *our men* would always wear Old Spice. To my knowledge Alex had never worn that scent, and I'd never told him that I loved it. Libby's Jason had worn it of course. She'd told me it was one of the signs that confirmed that he was so right for her. Libby and her signs.

"It's beautiful," I said. "Most of the lights on the evergreens

54

are completely covered. But the lamps on the lampposts, along the walk, show the trees up wonderfully."

From the dining room area, Bing Crosby sings "White Christmas". I'd always thought that song beautiful but sad, perhaps because it has to do with longing. I suddenly wonder about the days before my first Christmas. Where had I actually been? In a real home? Had someone sung a Christmas lullaby to me? Had I really been with a mother who had shortly afterwards given me away to strangers, sending with me only a wooden, jagged edged Christmas bell? My throat knots up.

"Miss Winfield," Bradley West said, looking at me closely, "a penny for your thoughts. You seem to be miles and miles from here."

Before I can say anything, and I'm glad because I don't know what to say, Hattie comes through the door, carrying a silver tray with slices of cake and steaming cups of coffee. "Hey, you two, coffee's ready." Scottie and Jude raise their heads off the rug, and Scottie begins thumping his tail. "Don't you dare," she tells him sternly. Both the dog and cat lower their heads to their paws.

Hattie places the tray on a coffee table in front of one of the couches. Two occasional chairs sit across from the couch. I head for the nearest chair, not wanting to go near the couch, in case Bradley West should just happen to sit there. You are acting like a silly schoolgirl, I think, but take the chair nevertheless.

Bradley sits on the couch next to Hattie. She serves the coffee and cake. I take a bite of the cake; it is rich and delicious.

"This is the best cheesecake I've ever had," Bradley said, between bites.

Hattie beams with pleasure at the compliment. "It's going to be great having you two here this Christmas season. It'll be the first time that I haven't been alone since Carl died, six years it's been." She looks towards the fire, a faraway look in her eyes. Her face has a soft glow about it now in the firelight. I wonder if she's seeing glimpses of Christmases past, perhaps happy times in this very room?

Bradley sets his cup and saucer on the coffee table. "Thanks so much, Hattie for the delicious supper, and the coffee and cake. I'm going to call it a night."

"Good night, Bradley," she said, looking up at him. "Sleep well."

"Glad to have met you Miss Winfield. Good luck on finding the origins of your bell." Then he strides across the room and disappears through the doorway.

"A wonderful young man," Hattie said, resting her head against the back cushion of the couch. "I never had children, but he would be one I'd be proud to call my own. He doesn't have any family in Colorado anymore, just a sister in California. He's divorced," she adds, like it's something I need to know. "He married young; it didn't work out. There were no children."

"I should go up to my room," I tell her, glad that she'd thrown in that little bit about Bradley West, wondering why I should care one way or the other. "I'm going to try for a goodnight's sleep and get an early start tomorrow and see if I can find out anything," I said, picking up my cup and saucer. "I'll help you carry these things into the kitchen."

Hattie rises off the couch, "It's been a long day for you as well."

We carry the dishes into the kitchen. I bid Hattie a goodnight and head towards the stairs. "Goodnight, dear, she said. "I enjoyed the evening very much."

As I go up the stairs, Bing Crosby is still singing softly, this time Silver Bells.

Back in my room, I draw a hot bath and pour in bubble bath. After I'd soaked until my skin is wrinkled, I dry off and slip into a pair of thermal pajamas. I brush my teeth, then turn off the bedside lamp. The room is in shadows. I look out the window overlooking Hattie's backyard. There's still a light on in the cottage. I sigh and go to bed and crawl under the quilts. I was spending way too much time letting this Bradley West character invade my mind, always seeing how that wisp of dark hair fell over his forehead, making me want to gently brush it back.

Soon, I'm warm beneath the mound of quilts. I put my hands

behind my head on the pillow and try to focus on what I can do tomorrow to move me closer to my goal, the reason I'm here anyway. Bradley had said that Sarah Fluty was out of town for a couple of days. I could go back into the shops in town, and show my bell, I hadn't felt comfortable doing that today. "And just why do you think you will be comfortable doing that tomorrow?" My own voice whispers through the darkness. What was I afraid of?

You have to stop this, I think, trying to will my mind into a more productive train of thought. But suppose I actually came face to face with the woman who had given me away? I should have a plan on what to say or do. Maybe I should make a list. What did I want from this journey? "Number one," I whisper, "I want to look into the face of the person who had given me away, to see if a little bit of myself is in her eyes, if her hair is auburn like mine, and maybe a bit curly and even more unruly if snow fell on it. Did the looks of some strange man ever make her shiver? "Damn!" I said, my voice seeming to echo in the darkness. There I go again letting this stranger into my head. Libby would probably say that it was a sign; she would tell me to just go with the little voice in my head. Libby always trusted her little voice. I'd trusted mine when it had said to follow the clues on the bell. What was it telling me about Bradley West? Perhaps nothing. Now back to what I want from this journey. Number two: Why had the bell been sent with me, and why only half? Number three: and I realized that this is actually number one, that it was what I wanted to know above all else, had she ever thought of me in all the Christmases that had passed since then, had I ever crossed her mind? That thought causes my throat to feel raw. I push the painful thought aside and instead see myself pushing away the wisp of hair off Bradley West's forehead.

Chapter Nine

I awaken to sunlight streaming through the window. For a moment I don't know where I am. Then my eyes fall on the bell on the nightstand. I must get going. After all, I only had a few days to find out if this journey was fruitful or futile. I brush my teeth and stare at my reflection in the mirror. Finding out who gave me my hair and eyes would be worth the journey, no matter who or what they turned out to be.

I'm starved by the time I get dressed. I look out the window. The snow with the sunlight glistening on it is beautiful, but blinding. I can't help looking toward the cottage and wondering if Bradley West is already in Hattie's kitchen eating hot rolls and drinking coffee?

I look at my watch, eight o'clock. Surely Hattie will give me breakfast, even if I'm a little late.

In the kitchen Hattie is standing by the sink smiling; by her side is a tall, thin man of about seventy-five, maybe eighty, wearing a red and black plaid jacket with matching cap with earflaps pulled down. "This is Frank," she said. "He's going to shovel the walk."

"Few more minutes, missy, and I'll have it all cleared out for you. I'll clean your car off, too."

"Thanks," I said.

He goes to the backdoor, picks up a snow shovel and opens the door. "You be careful out there, Frank. Don't fall down, you could break a hip," Hattie said.

"I'm spry as a young man, Hattie. Don't you worry none about me." But he seemed pleased that she was concerned and closes the door grinning.

"Frank is slow to get around sometimes. A few years ago he'd have been over here by daybreak and had the walks cleared by sunup. I guess we all get slower as we age. I'm not looking forward to that."

The warm smell of cinnamon rolls teases my nose and makes my mouth water.

"I've just taken my cinnamon rolls out of the oven," Hattie said, "Come on, have a seat there at the table."

The table is set for two. Will Bradley West be joining me? Or is the plate for Hattie? I sit, and Hattie brings over a platter of cinnamon rolls, the icing dripping down the sides. She places the platter on the table, then brings the coffeepot to the table, turns the cups upright, and pours the steaming, black liquid into both cups. "Bradley will be here shortly, she said. "Would you like orange juice? And bacon or ham, and eggs, anyway you like them, are on the menu."

"These delicious looking rolls will be all I need, thanks," I said, pouring cream into my coffee and stirring with a spoon.

"You going into town this morning?"

"Yes. I want to see if anyone has seen an ornament with a zigzag cut. I suppose it could be some sort of puzzle."

"Could very well be," Hattie said thoughtfully. "It could be that the other half is out there somewhere in this town,

A gentle rap comes from the backdoor. "That must be Bradley." She goes to the door, opens it and in walks Bradley West. He stomps his feet to shake off the snow and hangs his coat on a peg by the door.

There's that tingle again as I notice how handsome he is in a tan, crewneck, cable knit sweater over a white shirt. That lock of hair falls over his forehead as he takes the seat across from me. "Aren't you joining us, Hattie?" he asks. Leaving me to wonder if maybe he doesn't want to be alone with me.

"Maybe some coffee in a little bit. I ate hours ago."

Bradley takes a sip of coffee, looking at me over his cup. "What are your plans for today, Miss Winfield?"

"I'll be visiting the shops. Thought I'd ask if anyone has seen anything like my bell ornament."

"Do you think your bell was made here in Dell?" He asks, then takes a bite of cinnamon roll, waiting for me to answer.

"I'm almost sure of it. Dell Co. is written on the back."

"Why is the bell important to you?"

I hesitate. Did I really want to share with this stranger something so personal? I look into his eyes. He is waiting, questioning. What could it hurt? "It's the only link to my roots," I said softly.

"A mystery." he said thoughtfully, taking another sip of coffee. "Do you think it was mass-produced or was just one of a kind?"

Mass produced! I don't like the sound of that. It leaves me feeling a bit sick. Surely my bell was an original, created just for me. But suppose my birth mother....I didn't even know if she made the bell, I didn't even know anything at all really.

"Is something wrong?" Bradley West is asking, and I realize that I hadn't answered his earlier question.

"Just thinking. I actually don't know anything much at all about the bell, just that it was with me when I was adopted at three months old."

"And you want to solve the mystery of who placed the bell with you?"

"Yes. I want very much to know just that," I said a bit sharply, then quickly add, "wouldn't you?"

"Of course," he said. "How could anyone not do all they could to find the answer? I would like to see the bell, unless, of course it is too personal to share."

"I'd like you to see it," I said. "Maybe you've seen something like it. It's in my room," I said, rising from the table.

I get the bell from my room and when I get back to the kitchen, Hattie is letting the dog and cat in. Scottie shakes snow onto her floor. "Frank has the walk shoveled," she said, closing the backdoor. "Are you enjoying your rolls, dear?"

"They are wonderful, Hattie." I place the bell on the table next to Bradley. "I'm letting Mr. West look at the bell; maybe he's seen something while doing the craft interviews that will be a connection."

"Good idea," Hattie said.

Bradley picks up the bell and turns it over and over in his

hand, rubbing a finger along the jagged edge. "Interesting," he said. "Bailey," he reads from the back. "What does Bailey mean to you?"

"Nothing. I guess that it's someone's name. It could be a last name or even a first."

"True. And 1971?"

"The year of my birth."

"And Dell C O? You are positive that it means Dell Colorado."

"Almost. The only other thing I think it could be would be a company."

"Your parents didn't tell you anything about your history?"

"No. I think my grandmother arranged my adoption and she destroyed all the records."

"That is strange," Bradley West says, shaking his head. "One has to wonder why she would do something like that."

I'd wondered about that. Why would she do that, except to just wipe my slate clean? But burning my records didn't erase where I'd come from, who I'd come from. "There is so very much that I don't know, so little I do."

"I tell you what," Bradley said, handing the bell across the table to me, "I'll be interviewing Sarah Fluty tomorrow. She called a few minutes ago and is back in town. Come with me if you want, perhaps she would have a clue if you show her the bell. Maybe she'd know if someone in this area had done work of this type."

"Thanks. I'd like very much to go."

"Well, Miss Winfield. I've really enjoyed this talk, but I have to get back to work. I promised myself that I'd spend today working on the novel," Bradley said, rising from the table.

"Please, just call me Taylor," I said, wishing he'd stay a little longer.

He pours himself a refill of the coffee. "I consume far too much caffeine," he said laughing. "But I just can't seem to get the characters in my novel moving without it. You have a good day, Taylor. Let me know if you find out anything."

"Thanks. And good writing."

I watch him put on his coat, pick up his cup of coffee and go out the door, and I can't help noticing how broad his shoulders are.

I pick up the bell and stare at the shiny red paint. Who had painted it? What had she been thinking? Had she made it especially for me? Or had someone bought the bell then sawed it in two? Perhaps the scribbles on the back had no connection to me at all, but the date. The date of my birth, how could that not be connected to me?

As I start to leave the kitchen, Hattie sticks her head out of the pantry door. "You going into town?"

"Yes, in just a few minutes."

"They should have the sidewalks cleared by now. But it's going to snow again; the radio said two more inches. It's already starting to cloud up."

Just then the door opens and Frank steps inside, nods to me and calls to Hattie. "Hattie, I'm done now. But it's starting to spit snow again. I may have to come back this afternoon if we get what the radio said."

Hattie came out of the pantry, closing the door behind her, "You get yourself to the table, Frank. You need some hot coffee or cocoa to warm you up. And you are going to church with me this morning."

Frank grins broadly and heads towards the table.

"Would you like to go to church with us?" Hattie asks.

"Thanks, but I'm going to go into town."

"Some of the shops will open at eleven. Good luck, dear," Hattie said, as I went out the door.

Back in my room, I put on my coat and boots and go back down the stairs and out into the crisp December air. Clouds have covered the sun. My car is all clear of snow. Frank had said he would clean it off. And he's shoveled the snow from around it. What a nice thing for him to do. I get my camera from under the car seat, pick up my cell phone and go back to the room.

I find myself looking out the window and across the lawn to the cottage. What was he doing at this very moment? Creating people, places and things? What did he think of me, if anything? Why was I letting my mind run into such waters?

I'll get into town before the shops open and look in the windows before the crowds get there.

In the foyer, I pause for a moment and take the bell from my pocket. I rub my finger gently over it, wanting it to somehow have the magic to find its way back to that day some thirty years ago and take me with it, to observe the scene when someone tucked it along side a baby girl and sent them both on their way. Would that person have had a sad face, would she have had tears in her eyes? Or would she have been relieved to know that I was going, going forever? I suddenly think of Libby. I wish she were here. Tucking the bell deep into my coat pocket, I step into the chilly air and head for town.

The streets and sidewalks have all been cleared. Church bells chime, sending a lonely feeling through me. I can't recall a time in my childhood when my family didn't go to church on Sundays. When Grandmother Winfield was alive she insisted that all her family went and sat in the same pew, the Winfield family pew. There'd be Grandmother Winfield next to the aisle, next would be Uncle David and Aunt Kate, then my father and mother with me sitting between them. Had any of those people just once said, "*I don't want to do this today, this Sunday I'm going on a picnic or to another church.*" I close my eyes and picture Grandmother Winfield and I don't think anyone of them would have dared. Even after she was no longer in this world, the tradition had continued. I went away to college, and Mother stopped when Marcus came into her life. I imagine Aunt Kate is still in that pew on Sunday mornings.

Snow, that just minutes ago had been an occasional flake, is now many large flakes drifting down. I stick out my tongue, letting two large ones fall and melt, not caring who sees that I'm acting like a little kid. Only a few people are on the streets.

I stop in front of a window filled with handmade leather crafts: Belts, wallets, buckskin jacket with fringe trim, headbands, and several styles of boots: men, women and children's. A pair of low-cut brown ones makes me think of Alex. Two years ago I would have still been with him and would have certainly seen the boots as the perfect Christmas gift. I hope he finds what he truly wants under his tree this Christmas.

I look into the windows of several more shops, selling anything from birdhouses to saddles. Nowhere do I see one wooden bell. I turn down the side street, stopping in front of Barbara Benson's place, with the tree in the window containing wooden ornaments. What would it be like to come here late at night when all this was silent and still, just myself looking at the quaint little shops, with the soft lighting of the street lamps with the green garland and red bows. And I'd have snow falling softly. Maybe I would set up my easel. For an instant I imagine Bradley West by my side. "Getting entirely out of hand, girl," I whisper and try to get my mind to focus on the present. Libby would say go with the flow, just let your mind take you where it will. I say snap out of it. Get on with the task at hand. You didn't come to Dell Colorado to find a Bradley West.

The bells above the door jingle as it is opened from inside. The lady, who had been behind the register yesterday, looks out. "Hello," she said, smiling, then reaches back behind her, flipping the open sign around. "Isn't it beautiful out here?"

"Like a Currier and Ives painting," I said.

"I think so myself. Coming in?"

"Yes." I follow her back inside. "Are you the owner?"

"Yes, I'm Barbara Benson. I've owned this shop for the past fifteen years. Moved here from California. Came for a weekend and that was it. I had a shop in California, sold beachwear."

"None of that here," I said, looking out the window as the snow continues to fall, ever thicker now.

"None of that for sure," She said, just as the bells on the door jingle and two jolly faced, middle-aged women, in matching red wooly jackets come inside. They have identical features. Twins maybe, sisters not a doubt.

"Could I help you with anything?" Barbara asks, standing behind the cash register.

I reach into my pocket and pull out the bell, carefully laying it on the counter. "Have you come across anything like this?"

She picks up the bell and squints as she runs her finger over the jagged edge. "What is it? Some kind of puzzle?"

"I don't know for sure, but I think it's an ornament. A Christmas bell."

"I can see it could be that," she said. "But no. No. I've never seen anything like it. What does the writing on the back mean? Dell C O? Does that mean our very own Dell Colorado?"

"I think it does."

"Where did you get it?"

I really don't want to share my story with her and tell her it's a family item, and I would like to find out who made it.

She hands it back to me. "Sorry dear, that I can't be any more help to you. But I'll sure keep an eye out should anything like it come in here. Just leave your number."

I scribble down my cell phone number, and thank her. Then put the bell into my pocket. The two jolly ladies are at the counter, their arms loaded with items.

"Have a wonderful day and good luck," Barbara calls as the bells jingle as I open the door. I step onto the sidewalk as three more snow sprinkled customers go inside.

I go into five more shops; none of the clerks have seen anything like my bell. But all are friendly and wish me luck. One suggested that I go to Denver and check in the bell antique shop there. It could be a lead.

I stuff five dollars into a red kettle next to a bell ringing Santa. He smiles, and tells me, "Thank you, young lady." I guess even this enchanted place has its poor. Had the woman who had placed my half bell with me before she had given me away been poor? Was that why she had given me away? Was she homeless? Don't like to imagine that. I'm hungry--should have eaten another of Hattie's rolls. The hands on the clock in the tower of the courthouse point to one-thirty. I push open a door to Ruby's diner and stomp my feet on a black rubber mat that says Merry Christmas in bold red letters.

Jingle Bells is playing through a speaker above the doorway. The place is almost filled. A waitress in a red and white striped uniform shouts, "Three number twos." A sign instructs, "Wait To Be Seated". A young woman shows me to a table near the front window. "I'm Lori," she said smiling, laying a menu before me. Connie will be your server. She will be with you as soon as she can. It's so busy right now. We only have one table left. And I see two people waiting up front; we'll have to start taking numbers."

She hurries towards the couple standing beside the "Wait To Be Seated" sign.

Soon, Connie is there and takes my order. I just have a salad. I watch the people walking by; the sidewalk is becoming crowded. I wonder where they are all from, are most tourist? Most have red or green shopping bags with the name of the shop it came from: Sutton's Leather Crafts, Bob's Fine Pipes and Tobacco, Sally's Miniatures, Ruth Ann's Art, Jan's Book Store, Barb's Ornaments, and the list goes on.

I finish the salad and pay at the cashier desk. Several people are waiting for a table or booth. I step onto the sidewalk and join the flow of shoppers. The snow, falling finer now, stings my face. I pull up the collar of my coat; should have tried to find that knit cap. Maybe it's under the seat, or in that bag in the trunk of the car. Should be a shop that sells knitted items, haven't seen anything like that. I go across the street, walking between crawling traffic, thinking it would take a half-hour to just go around the courthouse in a car. I cross through the courthouse lawn, walking on the sidewalk that leads to the other side, cross the other street, with just as many crawling cars, and step onto the sidewalk in front of the Tribune. The closed sign is in the window. Could place an ad in the Tribune, have them take a picture of the bell. Don't think I could do that. If and when I find the person who placed this bell with me more than thirty years ago, I want to be able to see her first. I can't explain just why. Perhaps it is letting me have control of the situation, check it out, look before I leap thing.

There are fewer shoppers on this side of the courthouse. I step into a shop that has a wooden sign above the door that says: Harley's Fine Sausages and Cheeses. The shop holds much more that sausages and cheeses, any kind of cracker imaginable, and barrels of candy. A husky, bearded man is behind the counter, ringing up items for a customer. He sings out a cheery, "Hello."

I choose a chunk of Cheddar cheese, wrapped in red cellophane, and a small box of saltine crackers.

I'll head back to Hattie's. Going into the shops and asking about the bell had gotten me nowhere. Maybe I should just put the ad in the paper; again I don't have a good feeling about that. But I could ask at the Tribune, when they open tomorrow. Surely the editor would remember if such an item had ever been mentioned. And another idea just popped into my head, I wonder why I hadn't thought of it before. It had been done in countless movies I'd seen. Search back editions of the paper for clues. I could ask to see the issues of 1971, starting with September, going through December. My heart is racing. Maybe if my mother had intended to keep me when I was born, there'd be a birth announcement. Perhaps there'd be a Bailey listed. I find my feet are moving faster. I want tomorrow to hurry. I turn up the walk to Hattie's place. A car is turning into the parking area and parking next to mine. Bradley West gets out and disappears behind the house.

Chapter Ten

I walk around the side of the house to the parking area. My car is covered with snow again. Bradley West's footsteps have left long footprints in the snow going up to Hattie's backdoor. A good inch of snow covers where Frank had shoveled earlier. And the snow has almost completely turned to stinging pellets. I wonder if there is an ice storm in the forecast? I search under the seat for my hat, then open the trunk. Nothing. Maybe it's somewhere in all my stuff in Cincinnati.

Inside, in the foyer, I get a glimpse of myself in the mirror. I look a fright for sure. The snow has melted into my hair, causing it to be frizzy. Should have looked harder in town for a scarf or hat. Glad I didn't run into Bradley West. "Get a grip, Taylor," I whisper to my reflection; you really have to stop thinking about Bradley West. After all you aren't a silly teenager." I look deep into the eyes staring back at me from the mirror. "Who are you, really? Will you ever know?" I look at my lips and say the words, "Yes, I will know. I have to know."

Upstairs, I flop on the bed. It is made. Hattie had been in here and tidied up. Today, I had accomplished nothing. But I had a few more days here in this beautiful place, and Christmas was coming. And Bradley had promised that he'd take me along on his interview with Sarah Fluty. Didn't magical things happen at Christmas time?---well, in the movies anyway.

I soon drift into dreams in which a tall man with very wide shoulders keeps drifting in and out of the shadows; I'm trying to catch him to push back a wisp of dark hair. Then I see a young woman crying in the shadows, in her hands are two pieces of a broken bell. She tries and tries to fit the pieces together, but it's like a magnetic force keeps pushing the pieces apart. I jolt upright in bed, my heart pounding, my hands damp. The room is in semidarkness. I sit on the edge of the bed and push on the light on my watch that lets me see what time it is. Seven-thirty. I hug my arms tightly. The dream is still so clear in my head. Libby would say the dream was a sign. But of something good? I don't know. The woman's face was so sad. And why was I chasing Bradley West? The idea leaves me feeling a bit angry, and I laugh a bit nervously, after all it was only a dream. Only a dream.

Chapter Eleven

I shower and change into jeans and a cotton shirt, dry my hair, give it a few promises with the curling iron, dab on a few strokes of mascara, and brush a bit of powder over my nose. My stomach is telling me it needs food. Don't think the cheese and crackers will see me through the night. Maybe I'll try that Burger Palace down the street from the Holiday Inn.

The dream had left me feeling uneasy and I try to push it as far to the back of my mind as I can. I hear tiny taps on the windowpane. Sleeting again? I pull back the draperies. The railing around the balcony is covered with ice. Wonder how bad the roads are? Maybe if I hurry, I can get out to the burger place and back before it gets too bad. I put on my coat, grab my purse and car keys and go down the stairs and into the stinging sleet. No traffic on the street in front of the house. I slide and almost lose my balance. I creep to my car and find it covered in ice. Guess the cheese and crackers will have to do.

"Taylor." I look up. Bradley West is making his way towards me, looking more handsome than he had a right to, in a long tweed overcoat, a few balls of sleet glistening, clinging to that lock of hair.

Scottie wags his tail, thumping it wet against Bradley's leg. "Hattie wants you to come for supper. She saw you sliding down the walkway. I'd just gotten to her backdoor and she sent me after you. The roads are really bad. Hattie said she heard on the news that there have been several slide-offs. And it's going to get worse."

The thought of a hot meal is really tempting. I think of the alternatives, cheese and crackers. Cheese and crackers. "I'd be delighted," I hear myself say.

"I thought that Frank person said he'd be back to take care of the walks if needed," I said, taking a step away from my car.

"Let me help you," Bradley said, putting a gloved hand on my elbow. I get just a hint of Old Spice, and that, with his hand on my arm, gives me that darn tingle again.

I step onto the sidewalk and almost go down. Bradley steadies me with his hand on my elbow. "Careful," he said, holding my arm tighter.

"I've got my feet well planted, I think. I just wasn't prepared for it to be so slick."

"Here, loop your arm through mine," he said, bending his arm and holding it towards me.

I slip my hand into the crook of his arm; his coat feels soft and icy damp on my fingers. What had I done with my gloves?

Scotties lies down in front of us, rolls over, jumps back up, shakes his head, whines, then takes off across the lawn, his feet sinking through the crusted snow. A meow, as a black streak darts from behind a tree and races for Hattie's back step. Scottie takes long leaps through the snow and is soon beside Jude, waiting.

"I also wanted to tell you that the interview with Sarah Fluty is off," Bradley said, slipping just a bit, then steadies himself. "She had to go out of town."

"Is that going to cause you to miss your deadline?"

"No. She was kind enough to meet me in town and give me some articles and certificates that she'd gotten in school. I would prefer to have done the interview, but I think I can do the piece with what she gave me, and she brought a box of pictures. So, I should be able to put together a layout and meet the deadline without a problem. Sorry I didn't get a chance to ask about your bell."

"That's all right. Perhaps I'll get another chance before I leave," I said, hoping my voice didn't show the disappointment.

Hattie opens the backdoor, and the animals rush past her to get inside. "You two are tracking snow all over the floor. Get yourselves in there on your rug." But she's laughing, and I sense that she isn't at all upset about the floor. "You two, get on in here," she calls to us, holding the door a little wider.

As we get to the step, I find myself wishing we were going on a walk and that I could hold onto Bradley's arm and feel the movement of his body walking close beside me. I pull a little away, thinking that I'm letting my emotions or whatever take over. I can't

71

do that, can't allow that. Anyway, he's just being kind, doing Hattie a favor. And he probably has a girl friend. I let go of his arm and step into the warmth of Hattie's kitchen. Do I smell chili? I'm so hungry.

"You two sit. Sit there at the kitchen table. I'm just having chili and sandwiches and a fruit salad. I thought it would go good on a night like this. That ice storm came on so fast. Poor Frank, took a nap in his recliner and didn't even know it had happened. Poor dear, he said he'd come right over and take care of the sidewalks. I told him I couldn't be responsible for a broken hip and to stay put. Nobody should be out on a night like this, especially driving across town, and Frank has bad eyes at night."

Bradley helps me off with my coat and hangs it on a peg by the door, then takes his own off. We sit across from each other at Hattie's yellow and white checkered table. Hattie brings bowls of steaming chili on a tray with crackers and peanut butter sandwiches. She places a bowls before Bradley and me, then puts one at the end of the table. "I have a special treat," she said, going to the stove and removing an iron teakettle. She carries it to the table and pours steaming liquid into the cups. The spicy aroma of cinnamon fills the room. "Cinnamon tea." she said, setting the kettle on the sideboard then taking a seat.

"I'd like to say a little blessing," Hattie said, looking from me to Bradley.

"Sure," Bradley said, and I nod.

"Let us join hands," Hattie said, taking my left hand and Bradley's right. Bradley reaches across the table and covers my other hand with his. Hattie closes her eyes. "Thank you, Lord for these many blessings this Christmas Season. Thank you for these two young folks to share it with, for covering our little town with the magic of the beautiful snowfall. But, Lord, will you please send the Angels to melt the ice. It's dangerous trying to walk on it, could break an old hip." I look across at Bradley, I think he, as well as myself, find it hard not to at least smile at Hattie's words.

All through the meal, Hattie keeps us entertained with tales of Christmases of her youth in Kansas. I look at her and think what a wonderful life she's lived, what beautiful memories, then her next words makes me realize that when we judge someone we must think, could there be more, is there another side other than what they let us see? "I have some wonderful memories, to be sure," Hattie said. "But don't believe that all my memories are filled with sunshine, I've had my share of storms. But you know, without the storms in our lives, I don't think we'd really notice the sunny times as much. I guess the good Lord just slaps us with a bit of sadness ever now and then just so we'd know when we're blessed."

"I really like what you just said, Hattie," Bradley said. "Would you mind so much if I put that in my novel?"

"Hattie beams. "You have my ok."

After we'd eaten, and we'd thanked Hattie more than once for the delicious supper, both Bradley and myself start to help Hattie clear the table. "You two don't need to do this." Hattie said. "I'll clear all this up."

"It will take no time at all if we all pitch in," I said, taking a load of dishes to the sink.

"You are so kind to fix supper for us, and it was delicious," Bradley said, bringing bowls and glasses to the sink. In minutes, the table is cleared and the dishwasher is on.

Hattie puts on a pot of coffee. "Help yourselves when this is done, and there is cake in the cake plate, and I have plum pudding in the refrigerator. Eat all you want. But right now, I'm going to my bedroom. My favorite Christmas movie's on television. I've watched "It's a Wonderful Life" at least once each season for maybe ten or twelve years. Without watching that movie, Christmas just wouldn't be the same for me."

I feel a bit self-conscious when Hattie is gone from the room and I'm alone with Bradley West. You are so silly, I tell myself, letting this man make you feel like this. Maybe I should just go up to my room. Although, I didn't like to admit it, I wanted to find an excuse to stay, to listen to this man's voice, to look in his eyes, to hear what his views on life were. The little voice was telling me that I wanted to know everything about him, and I had to admit that it was true.

"If you are interested, I'd like to show you what I'm doing with my book," Bradley said.

"I'd like to see. The Crafters? Or the novel?"

"The Crafters. It's almost done. Hattie is letting me use the den to lay out my material on the big table she has in there. The cottage doesn't have a table, just a bar. Shall we?" he asked, leading the way out of the kitchen. The den is off the dining room. Bradley flips on a light switch to reveal a long table covered with papers and stacks of snapshots. "Hattie is a lifesaver, letting me use the table to sort through Sarah Fluty's papers and pictures. My story on her will start when she was a child and first learned she wanted to be an artist. You and she have a lot in common, you are both artists, and you have red hair."

Artist? He'd said artist, and I liked that. What would he say if he saw my paintings still stacked in storage in Cincinnati? Alex had said that they were nice. Just nice, not that they said anything to him or made him see what I was trying to say, or that they moved him in anyway. To Alex they were just pictures. What would Bradley West say if I should someday show him my creations? Would he see more than just pictures?

"She gave me so many pictures. When I'm faced with having to choose between so many, I find it hard to make a final choice. Another opinion helps, " Bradley said, jolting me back to reality. "I haven't gone through the pictures yet, just looked over some of these awards she got in grade school, seems Sarah's talent was known at an early age."

"How many pictures are you planning on putting in the piece about Sarah?" I ask, picking up a stack of snapshots.

"I'll have to limit it to five."

"How many people are you writing about for the book?"

"Twelve. There will be twelve in all."

"You have all the work done on the other eleven?"

"Yes. The publisher already has those and is waiting on this last assignment." Bradley said, picking up a snapshot. "As much as I've enjoyed working with these artists, I'll be glad when the last word is written and it's all in the hands of the publisher. Then I can work full time on the novel."

"You like working on fiction better?"

"I do. It's,"...he pauses and looks at me as if he is trying to find the words to tell me something that is very important to him. Maybe it's the same as when I tried to tell Alex about what my paintings meant to me.

"I guess with fiction I feel I'm creating something that otherwise would never exist," Bradley said.

"I know what you mean," I tell him, knowing I'm not just making idle talk, that I truly know. For a moment our eyes meet over Hattie's table. I look away, back to the snapshots in my hand. I'm feeling more and more for this man who I know so little about, yet feel oddly close to. I'm letting him get into my heart, and I don't even know if another holds his heart.

I'm looking at a black and white photo of a little girl of about six. She's holding a paintbrush, standing beside a building that has a few swipes of paint on the side. "This is adorable," I said, handing the picture across to Bradley.

Bradley takes the picture, looks at it and smiles. "I think that would be prefect in the beginning of the story. What I'll do is pick out the possible ones that could be used, then I'll just have to limit to the five best ones."

"Hard choices?"

"Sometimes."

The next picture causes my heart to leap. A little girl of about two or three is before a Christmas tree. But it isn't the child that my eyes are frozen on. On a limb of the tree among all the other ornaments, of balls and Santas and candy canes, is unmistakably half of a jagged, red bell. My hands are trembling; my mouth is dry. I don't speak; I just stare and stare.

"What is it?" Bradley asks, coming around the table to stand beside me. "Your face is white. What have you found?"

"My bell," I whisper in wonder and point to the spot in the snapshot. "It's the other half of my bell!"

Chapter Twelve

Bradley takes the photograph and looks at it closely. "Well, can you believe that? What are the odds? It looks like if you laid them side by side they'd fit together like a puzzle. Dang! I wish we could have gone out there and talked to Sarah."

You couldn't be wishing that more than I am, I think, but didn't say so. "Did she say when she thought she'd be back?"

"No," Bradley said, shaking his head. "It was an emergency with her husband's father. She didn't know how long she'd be gone."

"What about her mother? Wouldn't she know about the bell?"

"Mrs. Fleeming?" Bradley said. "I've met her, a nice lady. Sarah mentioned that her mother was out of town. Surely she'll be back by Christmas. She ought to know about the bell in the picture with her daughter. Could be a bell puzzle. Maybe, several were made and Sarah Fluty had one and you had a piece of one. I do hope it leads to your bell, Taylor. I surely hope it does," Bradley said, putting a hand on my shoulder.

"I hope so, too," I said. "Could I see the picture again?"

Bradley hands me the photograph, and I look and look. I wish I could take it back to my room and study it alone, but think it would be too much to ask him to let me have the picture. I bet he told Sarah he'd not let the material out of his sight. I don't want to put him in that situation.

"Don't worry," Bradley said. "Your answer will come. What ever it is you need to know, the answer will come."

"Thanks," I said, suddenly wanting to be alone, to sort out my thoughts. "I think I will just call it a night."

"Don't want to have some of Hattie's coffee and plum pudding?"

"No. I'm very tired. All that walking in town today and finding this picture. It's been some day."

"Have a good night," he tells me.

"You, too," I said. "You will work late here?"

"Yes, for a few hours."

I go into the kitchen and call to Hattie. "I'm going back to my room now. Thanks for the supper."

Hattie comes to the door. "Take some pudding."

"Thanks. It sounds delicious, but I'm stuffed.

"The movie is getting to the good part, where Jimmy Stewart realized the world wouldn't have been as good without him. That part makes me cry." Goodnight," she said, hurrying back towards her room.

In my room, I don't turn on the light, just go to the front window and look out. Sleet isn't beating on the glass. Maybe the storm is over for now. I look up into the sky. A few wispy clouds drift across the face of a half moon.

All this seems so surreal: the icy night, the moon, the clouds, and the handsome stranger just a floor away. The snapshot with what looked exactly like my bell hanging behind the little girl. What if the bell had just been a piece of a puzzle and several existed? If that were true, then my half bell probably wouldn't be connected to the one in Sarah Fluty's picture. Perhaps all this is really a dream and tomorrow I'll be thrown back into reality, and maybe I'll be back in Scalesville, or still in Cincinnati.

I feel so tired, so very tired. I go into the bathroom, turn on the light and prepare for bed.

I snuggle under the quilts. The half moon is shining on my face, giving way to shadows as clouds drift across it. Is Bradley West still in the room below? I imagine he'd looked again at the picture with the half bell. If I could look into the future, would Bradley West be on my life's road? "Silly, silly, girl," I whisper and sink deeper into the bed. I lie there in the shadows and think about what a remarkable day I'd just been through. To have seen the snapshot had to be more than a coincidence. Libby would say that my subconscious had willed it to be so. And maybe she would be right.

The moon is still playing hide and seek with translucent

clouds. I'm swept with a feeling I have no name for; it brings a memory of when I first remember seeing the moon. That moon had also been a half moon, seeming to dart in and out behind thin clouds. How old had I been? Three? It was before Grandmother Winfield took Boo away. I'd been in my bed and had suddenly awakened to moonlight shining on the bed. I'd been so afraid. I'd trembled under my blanket and clung to Boo. By some miracle, I'd overcome my fear, and by the time I started school and was reading about the universe from my father's massive library, I looked on the moon in awe and wonder and still do. But tonight, although it's not from fear, I have a feeling in the pit of my stomach that is akin to what I felt on that long ago night. Now, as was then, it's like something is missing.

Chapter Thirteen

If dreams came to haunt me, I had no memory of them. I awaken to a sunrise more beautiful than any I could remember.

The eastern sky is ablaze in orange. I get out of bed, wrapping the top quilt around me and go to the window. Clouds, like overhanging cliffs in a wonderful painting, are now turning from a brilliant orange to shades of purple and gold. The snow on the cottage rooftop is a soft pink. There are no lights on in the cottage. Is he standing at a window watching all this? What would it be like to share this with someone who saw the same beauty in it? I remember a sunrise almost as beautiful as this. Alex and I were in a little house in a Cincinnati suburb. I'd told him to get out of bed and look. He'd said, *"Good grief, Taylor, I've seen a sunrise before. If you've seen one, you've seen them all."* He'd pulled the covers over his head and gone back to sleep, while I had returned to the window and stared in awe until all the colors were gone. Alex had been wrong; each sunrise is a specialty all its own. Even as a child I had known that.

I stand there, wrapped in the quilt that smelled of Snuggles fabric softener, until the colors fade dim. Below, Scottie and Jude bolt across the lawn. Jude leaps delicately across the snow and is soon sitting on the lower limb of a naked tree. Scottie dashes across the frozen snow, breaking through from time to time, sinking up to his belly. I leave the window and step into the shower. As I shower, my thoughts are on the snapshot and the bell. Oh how I hope Sarah Fluty gets back in town before I have to leave, and that she will talk to me. With an ornament that unusual in the picture, she had to have at least have asked about it.

I blow-dry my hair, touch it up with the curling iron and dab on just a touch of makeup, didn't want to sit across from Bradley West and let him see me looking like a ghost. I'm spending way too much time thinking about what Bradley West might be seeing or thinking, I remind myself for about a half dozen times. I'll be gone from this place in just a few days. And Bradley and Hattie and this town will be just a memory.

I put on my coat and boots and go downstairs. I want to get the photograph album with my growing up pictures from beneath the car seat. I step into the clear, icy, December morning, gingerly making my way around the house to my car, sliding to my knees once. My breath steams out before me. Scottie comes to wag a welcome. I bend and give him a hug; he's warm under his thick coat; I can feel his heart beating. I've never had a dog of my own. I'd longed for one when I was about seven, but didn't dare ask. My mother was always talking about those nasty dogs of Mr. Hubbard's and how she'd never let such a creature in her house.

I retrieve the bag with the album from beneath the car seat. Scottie ran ahead, sat on Hattie's back step and waited. I decide to go in the backdoor. I can leave my snow-covered boots on the mat inside the door.

I tap lightly on the door and Hattie opens it. Scottie darts around her legs and runs inside. Jude comes from out of nowhere, whizzes through the door, disappearing inside. "Good morning, dear," Hattie said, holding the door wide. "Come on in. I have breakfast just about ready."

"Good morning, Hattie, " I said, stepping in to a wave of warm air. "What a beautiful morning."

"Did you happen to catch that glorious sunrise?"

I look towards the sound of the voice; Bradley West is leaning against the counter, a cup of something steaming in his hand.

"Yes, I saw it. It was beautiful," I said, laying the album on the small table, near the door, that held gloves and caps. I'm going to get me a hat or cap of some kind, I promised myself, wiggling out of my coat.

"I've never seen more gold in a sunrise. But then, they are all different you know," Bradley said.

I stare at him, and he looks back smiling, causing my heart to flutter wildly. I liked having shared something so beautiful with him, even though I hadn't been sure I was sharing at the time. I smile back, sensing that we'd shared a special moment.

As we ate a bountiful breakfast of bacon, eggs, sausages and pancakes, Hattie asks, "What are you two going to do this stunning day?"

"I plan to go to the newspaper office and see what I can find for the last half of 1971," I said. "Maybe I'll come across an article that will give me a clue."

"Good luck, dear," Hattie said, leaning over and squeezing my hand. "And you?" She asks, looking at Bradley.

I am wondering if he'd consider going to the newspaper with me and in the same instant, I realize that he probably is going to have to work almost day and night to meet his deadline. So much for that.

"I'm going to have to get on that last story for the book or I'm not going to make the deadline. And, Hattie," he said, putting a hand on her arm, "I really appreciate you letting me use the den. I hope it hasn't put you to a disadvantage, my having my things strewn all over the place like that. I'll have it all cleared out in a day or two. Once I get it laid out like I want, and decide exactly what I'll use, I can finish up in the cottage."

"Take as long as you like," Hattie said.

I want another look at the snapshot, just to reassure myself that I'd actually seen what I thought I'd seen last night. "Would you mind if I looked at the picture once more, before I set out for the Tribune?"

"Sure, look all you want," Bradley said, then added, "Perhaps you'd like to look through another envelope of pictures that Sarah gave me. I didn't realize I had it, until this morning. It was in among the papers."

"What are they of?" I ask, hoping there were more pictures of the bell.

"Family picture, I suppose. I really didn't see anything unusual. Nothing like the bell in the Christmas picture. But I may use one or two of them in the book. There are seven or eight."

"I'd like to see them."

Hattie looks out the window and smiles. "Frank is out there putting salt on the walk. Bless his heart."

Bradley and I take fresh cups of coffee into the den. I sit at the table and he takes the chair across from me. He picks up the picture with the bell in it, handing it to me. I hold it in my hands and stare and stare, wondering if I was actually looking at a bell that would, if I could just find it, fit mine. Am I somehow connected to the little girl in the picture? The pictures of me at that age look nothing like her, except for the red hair.

"I wish Sarah Fluty were here," Bradley said. "Taylor, I so much want for you to find your answers."

I trace with my finger over the bell in the picture and stare at the little girl. Did she know? So young. She wouldn't have understood if she'd been told. Now that Sarah Fluty was all grown up, would she know? Would she tell?

"I've been thinking," Bradley said, resting his hand on his chin and looking at me, "If I can get this wrapped up, and you take a break from your search, would you like to go skiing?"

I don't want to tell him that I've never been skiing, but I'd like very much to spend time with him. But he's going to find out that I don't ski when I fall on my butt. So, I said, "I'd like to go very much, but the only problem is, I don't ski, have never tried."

He smiles. "So. Everyone, who's ever tried, had a first time. I bet you'll do fine. Or maybe there is something else you'd like to do."

Was he asking me for a date? I liked that idea more than I wanted to admit. I reminded myself that in just a few days I'd be out of Dell Colorado, but the little voice in my head was beginning to sound much like Libby, saying take a chance, go with it. "Sounds wonderful," I heard myself say. "I'll have to be out of here before the New Year. I have my job waiting in Cincinnati."

"If you find what you're looking for here in Dell, would you consider staying?" Bradley asks.

"I hadn't thought about what I'd do really," I said, wondering why I hadn't let myself think beyond just finding out who had given me life? I pick up the pictures Bradley had just laid aside. I flip through them. Mostly groups of people. I can pick out the little girl who'd been beside the tree with the bell. I see pictures of her growing older, a teen, a young woman. These are all in color. Some are family pictures, Sarah's red hair standing out among the blacks, browns and blondes of others. Some of them have a woman who has white hair, although her face is young. I search for other redheads but find none. Was Sarah adopted? "What do you know about Sarah beside that she's a famous crafter?"

"Lot of tragedy in the family when she was a young child. Sarah's father was killed in a car accident when she was two. The accident almost took the life of her mother as well. The grandparents have passed."

"That's a sad story," I said, picking up the last photograph from the pile. "Will you try to dig deeper and find out more personal things to put in the book?"

"No," Bradley said. "This book is mostly about their lives now, when they knew they had talent, who influenced them, things like that. If they choose to share their most inner thoughts, well, yes, I would include that, but I wouldn't try to pull things out that they didn't really want to tell."

"Not like the National Enquirer?" I said teasingly.

Bradley laughs. "I know someone who works for them. He'll go to any length to get a story. He said he hid in a tree for a week on Tom Cruise's place, just to get a certain picture. And he digs through trash and garbage you wouldn't believe."

"Did he get it?"

"What?"

"Tom Cruise's picture. Did he get the one he wanted?"

"He did, else he'd still be in that tree."

I'm staring at a snapshot. The little girl of about seven is unmistakably Sarah. Four adults are in the picture, an older man and three women. One of the women is seated, maybe Sarah's mother? Although, her face is young, her hair is snow white. But it isn't Sarah, or the white haired woman that causes me to suck in my breath, I'm staring at the woman on the end. What was Grandmother Winfield doing in Sarah Fluty's picture?

83

Chapter Fourteen

I close my eyes then open them again. Was I letting my imagination go haywire? I stare again at the woman in the picture. It looks just like Grandmother Winfield standing slightly to the left of all the others, standing there staring right back at me. I'd been barely eight when she passed, yet I remember her face so visibly, the stern lips, the sharp chin, the dark hair. And there were also the pictures. I had one or two in the photo album. How could there be another person in the entire world with a face like that, perhaps once a beauty, but for some reason life had hardened her features? "Who is this?" I ask Bradley West.

Bradley takes the snapshot. "The child is, of course, Sarah Fluty; standing directly behind her are her grandparents, Henry and Emma Roland. The seated woman is her mother, and the other lady? Sarah wrote on the backs of all the pictures, identifying who is in them." He flips the photograph over. "Oh, here it is. Aunt Rett."

I take the picture back. "Aunt Rett!" I tap the image of the woman in the picture. "That woman is my Grandmother, Harriett Winfield!"

Bradley looks at me like he thinks I'm out of my mind. "You're kidding, right?"

"No. That is Grandmother Winfield. How did she know Sarah Fluty?"

"Maybe it just looks like your grandmother; people look like other people all the time."

"No. It's her. It's my grandmother Winfield." Aunt Kate had said something about Grandmother spending time in Colorado, didn't she say in nineteen forty something. But that would have been years and years before she was in this picture with a seven year old Sarah Fluty.

"My aunt told me that Grandmother spent some time in Colorado in nineteen forty something. See. She was in Colorado."

Bradley shakes his head. "Nineteen forty something? This

84

picture had to have been taken in the seventies. Sarah Fluty was born in sixty-nine." He rests his chin in his right hand. "How in the world is that connected? Think about it, Taylor. What is the connection? Could it be you want so badly to find the answer to where your roots are located that you are seeing more than what is really there?"

I stare at Bradley as a wave of anger sweeps hot through me. He thinks I'm a loose brain, inventing, like writing out a play, putting in the characters as I go. I rise from the table. "I want to find out where I came from. I want it very much. But I do not want it so much that I see what isn't there!"

Bradley holds up his hands. "Look, I didn't mean to upset you."

"You just wait," I said, rushing out of the room. I go to the kitchen, get the album and flip through the pages until I find a snapshot of the family at Christmastime, when I'd been about six. "There!" I almost shout, tapping the picture. Grandmother Winfield stares back at me.

"Are you all right?"

I look up to see Bradley standing in the doorway. "Look at this and tell me it isn't the same woman," I said, thrusting the album at him.

He takes the album and stares at the picture. "It sure looks like the same woman."

"It is the same woman. I know it!"

"Look," Bradley said. "I'm sorry if I said something to upset you."

"You didn't," I lie. "I'm going to the newspaper office. Maybe I can find out something in some of the old papers." I take the album and lay it back on the table.

"Good luck with the newspaper."

By the time I hit the sidewalk, my anger has cooled a little. Why had I become so enraged by his suggestion that I was seeing more into the picture than was really there? It had mattered more than I cared to admit what he thought. Maybe I thought he was seeing me as an impulsive woman grabbing at straws. That wasn't at all what I had become. Was it? Was it possible that I wanted so desperately to find clues that would lead me to the bell and to my roots that I was putting familiar faces on people in old snapshots? "Get a grip, Taylor," I said, then smiled foolishly, a woman bundled in a fur coat and hat, walking a dog that made them look like those "guess who's dogs this is" things, smiled weakly at me, with a look that said, poor thing.

I suppose it was possible for a woman in Sarah Fluty's picture to look like my late grandmother. The thing to do would be to have a talk with Sarah, find out just who this Aunt Rett person is, or was. I suppose she could be a little old lady that Sarah would let me meet.

The sidewalks aren't so crowded today. I decide I'd like Mondays in Dell Colorado. The sidewalks are clear, but mounds of snow are plowed between building and on the curbs. I just noticed something; I haven't seen one parking meter; wonder why I hadn't noticed that before? With all the traffic, it would be a good way to make a lot of money this time of year, but it would take away some of the charm of this place. Maybe that was just it, the town's people knew that already.

The sign on the Tribune's door is swung around to reveal the "Open" side. I push the door open and go inside to the jingle of bells, which are attached to a silken red ribbon hanging from the top of the door.

"May I help you?" a thin, balding man from behind a large desk asks.

"I hope so," I said, approaching the desk. "I'm Taylor Winfield from Indiana. I'm doing some research and was wondering if you have copies of your paper for all of 1971?"

"That we do, young lady," he said smiling. "The Tribune was started by my brother and me in 1954. We've kept a copy of each and every issue since that time. And before that when it was the Register, we have some copies, even some clean back to 1908."

"It's wonderful you saved all that history. But all I need is 1971."

"1971? he said, rubbing a hand across his chin. What

86

happened in 1971 that would make you come all the way from Indiana to look in our paper?"

I don't want to tell him that someone gave away a baby girl. He's staring at me, waiting for me to tell him about my important research.

"I'm looking for anything about the name of Bailey, either first or last name. And wondering if you'd seen anything like this," I said, taking the bell from my pocket.

"Don't remember writing anything about a Bailey," he said, getting up and coming from behind the desk. "By the way, my name is Daniel Slone," he said, holding out his right hand. I place my hand in his and he firmly shakes it. He takes the bell and runs his finger over it. "Nope, never seen anything like this. What is it, some kind of puzzle?"

"It's an ornament," I said. "I'm trying to find out if anyone in Dell made it."

"Could be. There are a lot of people in Dell who make things," he said, handing the bell back to me. "We keep all the old papers in the basement, this way," he said, walking towards a closed door. He opens the door to a stairs that goes down and flips on a light switch.

I hold on to a railing as we go down several steps into a large room with many tables with newspapers stacked neatly on top. To one side are giant rolls of white paper. On the wall are several shelves, each lined with stacks of newspapers. One small table with a chair is pushed against a wall.

"There will be a label on each shelf telling you what year. Help yourself and good luck. We sometimes get people in here doing genealogy, and we keep that one table there for anyone who might want to use it."

"Thanks," I tell him and watch him go back up the stairs. After his footsteps are silent, I stare at the stacks of newspapers and walk to the shelves. It doesn't take long to find the one with 1971 written in adhesive tape on the lip of the shelf. I carry a stack of papers to the table.

I look through all the birth announcements for September

1971. No girls at all for September 21st, my birthday. But suppose I hadn't really been born on September 21st, suppose that was just the date my parents, or more likely Grandmother Winfield, had given me? I find nothing that would connect with a baby being given away: no mentions of kids being taken from homes because of sickness or neglect. It is 1 p.m. by the time I've scanned all the papers for 1971. Time wasted. I sigh and place the stack of papers back on the shelf. It looked like my only lead was Sarah Fluty. Hopefully she'll return to Dell and agree to talk to me before I had to leave for Cincinnati. I had to get back to work; else I'd be penniless and homeless in a few weeks.

"Find what you were looking for," Daniel Slone calls to me, as I come up the stairs into the newspaper office.

"No. I didn't find anything. But thanks so much for letting me see the papers."

"Sorry, you didn't find anything, but good luck in whatever you're searching for. And a Merry Christmas to you."

"Thanks," I tell him and step out into the frosty December air. The sun is completely hidden now, and a few snowflakes drift lazily down, some landing on the brown coat of the man walking in front of me, his arms loaded with gaily-wrapped packages.

I stop in front of a jewelry store. Christmas in three days. I go inside. Hattie had worn a charm bracelet that first evening. The lady behind the counter smiles and asks if she can help me. "I'd like to see what you have in charms, dogs and cats."

She shows me several, and I pick one of a dog that looks a lot like Scottie, but can't find one of a cat anything like Jude. "Would you consider a brooch?" she asks, going to a small display case on the counter. She pulls out a gold colored brooch with a dog and cat nestled together on a rug, in small lettering the word *Friends*.

"Perfect," I said and forked over more money than I'd intended. An item on the back shelf catches my eye: A sign, gold lettering on black, "Writer at Work". "I'll take that sign." I tell her, pointing.

She puts both items in gift boxes. "Would you like these gift-wrapped?"

"No. I want to do that myself."

"I'll put in some paper and ribbon if you like."

"Yes, that would be perfect."

I go outside and stop in at a diner. Although, it's past lunchtime, the place is crowded. The hostess finds me a small table near the back. The waitress, perhaps nineteen and at least six months pregnant, comes and takes my order. I order a tuna salad on rye and a coke. "I'll be quitting work when the baby comes," she volunteers. "Hank, that's my husband, got a new job last week."

"Congratulations on the baby," I said, staring at her earrings, tiny wooden bells. "Your earrings? Are those handmade?"

"Aren't they lovely?" she asks, touching the right one. "And yes, they are handmade. Sarah Fluty made them; maybe you've heard of her. She's famous, makes all sorts of tree ornaments, and she started making jewelry also."

She looks towards the counter. "Well, better get cracking, the manager is giving me the evil eyes," she laughs. "Doesn't like for us to spend too much time chatting. "But if you want some earrings, similar to this, she's coming out with a catalog next year, course they wouldn't be exactly like these, all her stuff is one of a kind."

When I get outside, the snow has turned to rain. I duck my neck into the collar of my coat. Should have tried to find that hat. I'll be drenched and frozen by the time I get back to Hattie's. I'm already shivering. I start walking faster as the rain begins falling harder. An old blue truck pulls up to the curb, and the window rolls down, "Hey, there, Miss, ain't you staying at Hattie's place? Get in before you get soaked," Frank, Hattie's handyman said, pushing the door open.

I climb inside. "Thanks for stopping."

"Well, it's a good walk back to Hattie's place. That where you wanta go?"

"Yes, I need to get back there."

As the windshield wipers swish back and forth, Frank tells me he does lawn work on this part of town, summer and winter.

"Mow in the summer and shovel in the winter, it keeps a fellow busy."

By the time we pull into Hattie's drive, I know that Frank was married to the same woman for fifty years, has been a widower for three, that he has five sons, two daughters, and seven grandchildren. "They are scattered all over the country now," he said, as I got out of the truck.

"Thanks so much for the ride."

He climbs out also. "Bet Hattie has a cup of that hot cider," he said. We walk to the backdoor, and Frank raps three times and grins at me. "Hattie will know my knock".

Hattie opens the door, and the way she smiles at Frank leaves me wondering if they are more than just friends? "Lands sakes, you two, get on in here out of the weather," she said, opening the door wide.

She tells Frank that she has hot cider for him and asks me to have some also. I make an excuse that I need to dry my hair

I see myself in the mirror in the foyer. My hair is plastered to my head. I take off my damp coat and head up the stairs. In my room, I retrieve the two gifts and my bell from my coat pocket, lay them on the nightstand and hang the coat on the back of a chair. I sit on the edge of the bed and take the gifts out of their boxes. I'd bought the brooch for Hattie because she'd been so nice to me. I pick up the Writer at Work sign. I'd bought that for Bradley West because? Because? I don't know from what because. What reason would I have for giving this stranger a Christmas gift? What would he think? The last time I'd seen him, I'd gone away angry, because he'd suggested that I was seeing more in the Sarah Fluty photographs than was there.

I take a bath, wash my hair and dry it with the hairdryer, then plug in the curling iron. I dress in navy sweats and go to the window. A light is on in Bradley's window. The rain is falling harder now, turning the snow to slush. Frank's truck is still in the parking area.

I'm going to have to find that grocery store or a McDonald's or something. I'm getting hungrier by the minute. I do have some of that cheese and crackers from yesterday, but it wouldn't be near enough. I touch up my hair with the curling iron and dab on a bit of makeup. My coat is still damp. I discard the idea of trying to dry it with the hairdryer. It would only get wet again. I put it on and head down the stairs.

Hattie comes into the foyer. "Hi. I was just going to come up and ask you to come to supper. It'll be ready in about an hour. I've made a big pot of vegetable soup.

"Thanks, I appreciate the invitation, but I'm on my way to the grocery. I'll pick something up while I'm out.

Hattie insists that I take a yellow umbrella she gets from the closet by the door.

When I get to my car, I find a trench coated Bradley West opening the door to his car. His hair glistens in the light shining from the light next to Hattie's backdoor. Doesn't he ever wear a hat? Maybe he's just like me, thinks about buying one only when the need comes up.

"Any luck in your search," he asks.

"Nothing." I tell him.

Thinking that he's going to be soaked if he doesn't get into his car, I say, "Have a good evening."

I fold the umbrella and grab the door handle. My hand slips off, wet with the icy rain. I shake my hand and try again. Where are my gloves, under the car seat? Back in Cincinnati? I finally get in and turn the key, the motor hums. I turn on the heater. "Dummy," I whisper, when a blast of cold air hits me in the face. "You know you have to wait until the motor heats up. What is wrong with you anyway?" I look to my left; the reason is just a dark blur through the raindrops on my car's window.

I turn on my lights, back up, head out of Hattie's parking area, turn on the wipers and head north.

I snake through traffic on the main street. Wouldn't you think the rain would keep shoppers inside on a night like this? The parking lot at the milk barn is almost full; customers are darting in and out the door, racing for the door of the building or back to their cars. I park and dash into the building. I purchase an orange, a giant red apple, a bunch of grapes, a ready-made salad from the deli, and a soda.

As I pull into Hattie's driveway, I notice that Bradley's car is gone. Frank's truck is still there.

I grab my packages, unfold the umbrella and make a run for Hattie's front door. The rain is really coming down. Perhaps Dell Colorado won't be having a white Christmas after all. I feel a little sad with that thought. Seems like a place like Dell Colorado should always have a white Christmas. I've never seen a Currier and Ives Christmas card with rain on it.

Chapter Fifteen

After I've eaten. I slip into thermal pajamas and terrycloth slippers, turn off the light and stand in the shadows by the window, sipping soda. Frank's truck is gone. Bradley's window is dark, and his car isn't in the parking area. Why did I care? Would he notice if mine wasn't in the parking space? What I really need to do is get a good night's sleep. Maybe in the morning my brain will be working better.

I climb into bed, pick up my cell phone and dial Libby's number. She answers on the third ring. "Hi, Lib. It's Taylor."

"It's about time you called. I've been worried, and each time I tried to call you, I got this irritating recording saying that the party you called isn't available. What's going on? What did you find out about the bell? Have you met someone special? Tell! Tell all," she said in one breath.

I tell her about Bradley West and that he smells like Old Spice; that he likes sunrises. I tell her about Hattie and Scottie and Jude, and that Dell Colorado looks like a painting on a Currier and Ives Christmas Card. I tell her about the pictures, the one with the half bell, and the other one with someone who looks exactly like Grandmother Winfield.

"Oh, Taylor, this is all so exciting, I can hardly stand it," Libby said. "Are you writing all this down? You should be journaling, you know."

"No, I haven't written anything down yet. Look, I don't want to take up any more of your time. Take care and have the greatest Christmas ever."

"We are leaving in the morning for Jason's parents and will be back the day after Christmas. Can you call me then and tell me what happened? You are going to have a wonderful Christmas,

Taylor. I just know it. It's going to be the best you ever had. I'll be wishing really hard for you to find where the bell came from. And it will happen for you. I know it will."

After I hung up, I lay in the darkness hoping she was right, that I would find where the bell came from, find the other half to make it whole, to make me whole. And what if I didn't? What if the other half wasn't anywhere in Dell Colorado or anywhere in the world for that matter? I would go on, have a life, this much I knew. But I would always be wondering who had given away their baby girl, and why? I fell asleep to the rain falling harder, beating against the windowpane.

Chapter Sixteen

I awaken to the stillness of that gray time just before dawn. What is today? The day before Christmas Eve. I lie there in the shadows, warm beneath my mound of quilts. I don't hear rain. Perhaps it has turned cold enough to snow? It should snow on Christmas. It really should snow at Christmastime in a place like Dell Colorado. I think about the gifts I'd bought for Hattie and Bradley. I plan to give Hattie hers sometime tomorrow, or maybe wait until Christmas day. But I don't know about giving a gift to Bradley. Would it be appropriate? Shouldn't have been so impulsive and gotten it in the first place.

I crawl out of bed and go to the window. It's almost dawn now. Bradley's window is dark. The rain from last night has melted most of the snow. A slight mound of white is against the neighboring fence, and along the walk where Frank had shoveled are a few patches. Scottie and Jude dash across the walk. Jude runs up a tree, and Scottie disappears on a run behind the cottage. Looks like it will be a cloudy, if not snowy Christmas. What had it been like that Christmas of thirty years ago for the people who had given away a baby girl? Did they wonder what kind of Christmas was being celebrated where she was? Did they wonder in the years since? Then there is the possibility they had tragically died, and that was the reason for the giveaway. But if that had been the case, why would Grandmother have destroyed my records? Why would she have thought it necessary to sever all traces of my past, if I didn't have one? A mystery to be sure, Libby would say, and that all mysteries could be solved. I wish she could solve this one.

I dress in jeans and a white, boat-neck, pullover sweater. I'm looking forward to Hattie's homemade hot chocolate. And perhaps Bradley would be having breakfast with us.

When I get down to the kitchen, Hattie is at the backdoor letting the dog and cat inside. "It's cold as Christmastime out there for sure," Hattie laughs, closing the door. "Good morning to you, dear. Go ahead and sit at the kitchen table. The hot chocolate is ready and breakfast will be, just as soon as the biscuits come out of the oven."

"Good morning, Taylor," Bradley said, coming through the French doors, a newspaper in his hand.

"Good morning," I said, wondering if he'd been in the den working for hours on his book. "How's the Sarah Fluty story coming along?"

"Very well. I'll have it done before the first of the year."

"You two, sit, sit," Hattie said, waving us towards the table. I take a chair, and Bradley sits across from me, laying the paper behind him on a small table. But not before I saw a full-page announcement on the back, in red and green ink: "Community Celebration. Come one. Come all. Let all of Dell Colorado come and rejoice at this Christmas Season at the Community Center, on this day before Christmas Eve. 6.P.M. til?

Feeling his eyes on me, I try to think of something to say and blurt out, "So, are you going to the Community Celebration tonight? I saw the announcement on the paper there."

"Wouldn't miss it. You must come, too."

"I...I don't know," I mumble.

"Of course you'll go," Hattie said, placing a huge tray filled with eggs, sausage, bacon and pancakes on the table. "It's a wonderful celebration. And almost everyone in Dell will be there. The first celebration was held more than a hundred years ago. You can't miss this."

"Ok," I said. "What does one wear to this celebration?"

"What ever you feel comfortable in. Dig in, dig in," she said, turning her attention back to the table. "Everyone should eat a hearty breakfast. And tonight, there'll be a big dinner at the community center. The Masons are providing the food."

Just then three raps on the back door. "That's Frank," Hattie said, smiling."

As Hattie goes to open the door, Bradley winks, leans towards me and whispers, "I think Hattie has a beau."

"Sure feels like Christmas out there," Frank said, coming inside and taking off the checkered coat and matching hat. "Slick as glass out there. Smells wonderful in here, Hattie," he said, smoothing his wavy white hair with a large hand.

"You shouldn't be out on ice, Frank," Hattie said.

"Wanted to see if you needed anything."

"You'd better be hungry," she smiles at him, her cheeks flushed. I think Bradley West is right about that beau thing, and that makes me smile. Frank and Hattie seemed exactly right. A perfect fit, Libby would have said, and would have added that it was all in the plan of things.

Frank smiles and tells us good morning as Hattie leads him to the table. "You sit right here," Hattie said, patting the back of a chair.

"We're gonna get a white Christmas," he said, sitting down and scooting up to the table. "Just heard the weatherman on the radio say so. Said it will start to snow by dark."

"Wonderful," Hattie said, sitting down. "It always adds something special to a Christmas when it's white."

Frank fills his plate high with pancakes, tops them off with a large spat of butter, then pours maple syrup over them. "Nothing like Hattie's pancakes," he said, to which Hattie beamed.

"By the way," Hattie said, turning to me, "at midnight on Christmas Eve some of the residents of Dell welcome in Christmas with a church service. You will come, won't you, dear? It's such a beautiful service. It's held in the oldest church in Dell. Non-denominational. It doesn't matter what one's specific beliefs are, just so long as they believe in something greater than themselves."

"Sounds wonderful," I said.

"I'm not a religious person so to speak," Frank said, letting his eyes travel from me to Bradley. "I'm a spiritual person, just don't believe in any particular religion, but I like going to that old church at midnight on Christmas Eve. There's a certain magic; you can feel it. It's like the feeling is rising out of that old rooftop and going out there to bring peace to all the world. I tell you in that one moment at midnight, just as Christmas comes over the world, I'm filled with awe." The three of us are silent. I don't believe anyone of us, not even Hattie, had expected something so deep to come out of this simple looking old man.

Hattie places her hand atop his leathered, and slightly gnarled one. Bradley nods his head, "Well-said, Frank."

"No place on earth like Dell at Christmastime and being with those you love," Frank said, looking adoringly at Hattie. Hattie looks at him, and I see the shared look that passed between the two of them.

Fifteen minutes later, I'm back in my room. I wrap the two gifts and put them on the nightstand. Hattie had said that today the shops would be open until five, then til noon tomorrow and then would close until the day after Christmas.

I wanted a tiny Christmas Tree and a few decorations. If I hurry maybe I can find a tree lot that hasn't sold out.

I hurry out into the blistery air, telling myself that I just had to find a hat. The walk is just a bit slippery; guess Frank hadn't put out salt yet. After a great deal of scraping, I'm able to see out the windshield. I hurry my car onto the street, almost sliding into the curb. A salt truck creeps by, spraying salt onto the street. I manage, not without a great deal of spinning tires, to drive the car in behind the truck. I follow the truck past the milk barn and stop at a lot that announces "Dell Lion's Club Christmas Trees." The lot is surrounded by a string of light bulbs. A small camper sits in the center of the lot, with an "Office" sign in the window. The lot is almost bare; all that's left are two tall, scraggly, ice-crusted pines, and one two-foot fir, missing about half its branches. It sits all alone, abandoned about twenty feet into the lot, a tiny stand nailed to its bottom. Had anyone considered taking it home? Would even Charlie Brown have wanted it? Maybe not. But I do. A red tag is tied to the top: $4.95. I pick it up, try to shake off the ice and take it towards the office. By now a skinny man in a tan ski jacket comes towards me. "Want that little one?" he asks smiling.

"It's Perfect," I said, reaching into my purse.

"No charge." The man said. "You take it on home and have your best Christmas ever, you hear."

"Thanks so much. And you and your family have a great Christmas, too."

I put the tree into the back seat and look back; the man is standing next to the scrawny pines. Wonder how long he'll stay there, if no one takes those pines?

I park my car at the curb in front of Helen's Fine Knits, get out and go inside. Two other customers are inside. "Thirty percent off everything in the store today," a gray haired woman, behind the counter, tells one of the customers. I select a brown knit hat that has a narrow floppy brim.

"Find everything you wanted?" The lady asked, ringing up my purchase.

"Yes, thank you." I notice her nametag is Helen. "Did you make the hat?"

"I did." she turns the hat inside out, exposing a small tag. "Look here," she pulls the tag towards me. "You can always tell a Helen Smith creation by the tag inside.'

Printed on the tag is: "Created by Helen Smith. Dell Colorado." I nod and take money from my purse.

"I'll just wear the hat," I said, when she started to put it into a bag."

"You'll need it as cold as it is getting outside," she said, handing the hat back to me.

I removed the price tag and put the hat on my head.

"Perfect," Helen Smith said.

Outside, I head down the street towards the ornament shop. The giant clock on the courthouse points to eleven. I pick up my pace, feeling snug and warm inside my coat and Helen Smith's creation on my head. Only my nose is cold, and I bet as red as Rudolph's.

From the ornament shop, I choose a dozen, tiny, wooden balls of green and red with gold and silver stars, a dozen stars painted solid silver, and a box of white, miniature lights. When I get to the counter, I notice a small wooden angel on a shelf behind the cashier. "The angel? Isn't that handcrafted?"

"Absolutely," Barbara said, reaching behind her, taking it off the shelf. "All our items are handmade." She holds out the angel. "This is the last of the angels. A Sarah Fluty creation."

"It's lovely," I said, looking at the delicately crafted wings, thinking it would be perfect to top off my little tree. "I'll take her."

"Any luck with finding out about your bell?" Barbara asks.

"Not yet."

Hattie grins as I come through the door with the tree. "Where did you get that?"

"At the Lion's Club Lot. Do you have a box or something I could set it on?"

"Take the little table that's sitting up there in the hallway."

"Thanks Hattie," I said, lugging the tree and bag of decorations up the stairs.

I get the table from the hallway and place it before the window overlooking the front lawn, set the tree on it and begin to decorate. When I'm done, I plug in the lights. To me it's beautiful. I look out the window; Bradley is coming up the front walk. He looks up and waves. I wave back, wondering if he thought me foolish, putting a tree in my room when Hattie has two downstairs, and why it mattered what he thought? I place the two gifts under the tree. I look out. Bradley is gone.

Chapter Seventeen

I lie on the bed. I'm looking forward to the evening. Maybe Sarah Fluty would be back in town and be there. And Bradley West would be there. That chill again. Libby would say it was a sign, my little voice telling me that wonderful things were on the horizon. But my own rational mind won't let me feel that for long before it's saying, but what if it's a warning of something not so wonderful on the horizon? I know I'll enjoy the evening a whole lot more if I just go with Libby's way of thinking. "It's Christmas time, Taylor," I whisper into my pillow, "Just for this Christmas, just feel the joy and goodwill that's all around this town, these people, become part of it for one special Christmas season and see where it goes."

I doze off, to dream of Bradley West sitting on a white horse, holding up half of a red Christmas bell. He looks at me then gallops off into a snow-filled forest of evergreen trees.

When I awaken with the dreams still vivid in my mind, I tell myself I'll have to tell all this to Libby as soon as I talk to her again. She thinks dreams are messages from our subconscious.

Hattie had said to wear anything. I'd picked out dark green flannel slacks and a lighter green sweater set. Mother told me once that I looked lovely in green. I stare at the tiny tree and feel such sadness as I think of her. She would have thought my little tree unworthy of decorating, never seeing the simple beauty in it. With a heavy heart, I recall the few times I'd brought my artwork home. She'd said, "How nice", but had never hung one on the refrigerator like Libby's mom always did. She'd stuck them in a drawer someplace. Once I found three of them in the trash. What had she really thought of me?

Even though my mother had been cold and distant to me, I feel in my heart that she had cared, she had to have cared to have kept the bell. And then to tell me about it. To give me the only hope, the only clue to who I am. "Thank you, Mother," I whisper. "Thank you for giving me that. I'm sorry life didn't bring you whatever it was you wanted." I sank to the floor by the tiny tree and let hot tears run down my face. I cried for my mother and her lost dreams, and I cried for a little girl who grew up longing for something she didn't have a name for.

After I'd cried until no more tears came, I got up and went to the bathroom. The face looking back at me from the mirror is tear-stained and streaked with mascara, the eyes red and puffy. I splash cold water on my eyes, then dig into my makeup bag and get a jar of cold cream and apply it to my face. In minutes, my face is sparkling clean, but my eyes are still red. I find a bottle of Visine and squirt three drops into each eye. Just as the advertising had promised, the red is gone. But my eyelids are still puffy. If I'm lucky that too will be gone by the time I get dressed to go to the celebration. I don't want Bradley West wondering about why I'd been crying.

By the time I apply fresh makeup, the puffiness is all gone. I take extra care with putting on the makeup and feel a bit uncomfortable when I admit to myself that Bradley is the reason for the extra care.

At five-thirty I go down the stairs, my coat and hat in hand. Hattie and Frank are in the foyer with their coats on. "I was just getting ready to come up and see if you were ready," Hattie said.

"Need to get there a bit early," Frank said. "Wanta get the best table.

The front door opens, and Bradley, strikingly handsome in a gray tweed overcoat, the collar turned up against the biting cold, steps inside. His head is bare, a few snowflakes cling to his dark hair, and he is shivering.

He pushes the door closed behind him. "It's just started to snow."

"Told you we were gonna get a white Christmas," Frank said.

"Hattie," Bradley said. "I turned the car on so it can be warming up for you."

"Thanks so much, Bradley," Hattie said.

"I could've done that for you, Hattie," Frank said.

"I know you could've and I appreciate it, but Bradley already had his coat on and everything. And sometimes it is good to let young folks do things.

"Ride to the festivities with me?" Bradley asks, looking into my eyes.

"I would like that," my voice said; my heart said I'd like that *very* much.

I start to put on my coat, Bradley takes it out of my hands and holds it while I slip my arms into the sleeves. I turn around and meet his eyes. I look away, reminding myself that in just a few days I would be gone from this place, and Bradley West would be just a memory. Libby would have said, Oh, but, make it the best memory, a memory that will last a lifetime. I look again at Bradley and believe it would be easy to make a memory that would last a lifetime.

"You look lovely, Miss Winfield," Bradley said teasingly as we step onto the porch.

Now, who calls anyone Miss? Libby would love it, saying that Bradley West is a gallant gentleman. "Better take my arm, the walk is just a bit slippery," he said, extending his arm.

We walk to his car, which is running. I like that he's warmed up the car.

He opens the passenger side door, and I slide into the seat. He goes around and gets inside. Hattie and Frank, with Frank at the wheel, are already pulling onto the street. The snow has started to come down harder. Bradley turns on the wipers. As we pull into the street I said, "It is kind of you to drive me."

"My pleasure," he said, looking at me.

When we get to the parking lot of the community center, the area is full of cars. Bradley helps me out of the car. I take his arm as we walk to the door. Bradley opens the door to "White Christmas" playing softly.

We step into a large, warm room filled with a noisy crowd of men in flannel shirts and crew necked sweaters, women in reds and greens, and brightly dressed children rushing about. Hattie and Frank are waiting by the door and lead us to a table.

Frank holds a chair while Hattie sits, then sits down next to her. Bradley pulls out a chair next to Hattie and I sit; he sits next to me.

"Everything looks lovely," I said, noting the large red and white bells hanging from the ceiling. The tables have red and green tablecloths, along with centerpieces of large red candles and holly.

"They go all out," Hattie said.

In an adjoining room, a tree reaches to the ceiling. It is adorned with multicolored lights, garland and tinsel, and a woman with snow-white hair, dressed in a green dress, is putting ornaments on it.

A man in a red sweater goes to a podium; the crowd hushes as he begins to speak, "As most of you know, I'm Mayor Bannon, and I want to welcome all of you who have come out on this wintry night to join in the celebration. And that snow out there really is beautiful." To which everyone claps. "Thanks to the Masons for the food," he continues. "And we have a special program featuring the East Side Elementary School children singing Christmas songs. Everyone have a great evening and Merry Christmas one and all." He sits down. And children dressed in green and red robes line the stage and begin singing "Here Comes Santa Claus, followed by "Rudolph The Red Nosed Reindeer". After catching their breaths, they bellow out "Joy To The World". Then they bow as everyone claps.

"Wonderful children," Hattie said. "And there will be a present for everyone under the tree in there;" she gestured towards the tree in the next room. "It's been that way for over a hundred years."

I look towards the tree, wondering how the gifts for the children have changed over the years. The white haired woman in the green dress is gone.

The mayor returns to the podium and reminds everyone that

the children will all get a gift after dinner.

A chubby man with a white beard, who I thought would made a great Santa, takes the podium, announces that he is Brother Simms and asks us all to stand in prayer. We do, and he gives a lengthy prayer. When he is finally finished, Frank whispers to Hattie, "Bout time."

Soon, waitresses and waiters are taking our orders. We have a choice of a turkey or ham dinner. I choose the turkey. We are soon enjoying a delicious meal. Hattie and Frank begin telling stories about earlier happenings at long ago Christmas gatherings. As Bradley and I listen, I wonder if he's picking up tidbits to put into his novel?

"Remember that time it was Hazel Worthington's turn to decorate the tree and she put real candles on it and one of the Hadley boys got in there and lit several and caught the tree on fire. Luckily Hollis French was standing nearby and was able to grab the fire extinguisher." Frank laughs, "I don't think that kid sat down for a week, but we did get a rule out of it: no more real candles on the tree."

"This is all so wonderful," I said. "I can just feel the warmth and goodwill embracing this whole building."

"Doesn't it all make you just want to stay in Dell?" Hattie asks.

I nod. "All I've seen since I've been here is almost like something you'd read about in a book."

Hattie smiles and nods. Waitresses and waiters are clearing the tables as most people are done eating. I excuse myself and head for a hall leading towards the back. An arrow points to a sign marked "Rest Rooms".

I freshen up my lipstick, powder my nose and then head back to the table. When I get to the doorway to the room with the tree, I remember Frank's story about the candles. I stop and stare at the tree. It is lovely. And on getting closer, I see that the decorations, except for the garland, tinsel and lights, appear to be made of wood. I step closer, wondering if it's a Sarah Fluty creation? The white headed woman decorating the tree? Was she in the picture with a young Sarah Fluty?

I step inside for a closer look. I reach out my hand and examine a small red ball, much like the one on my Charlie Brown tree back in my room. But it's what I see when I move a step to the other side of the tree that almost makes my heart stop. I put my hand to my throat as a gasp escapes my lips. There, just inches from my fingers, hangs the other half of the bell! My bell!

Chapter Eighteen

I stare at the half bell on the beautifully decorated tree, a knot in my throat. I reach towards it, my fingers trembling. I'm almost afraid to touch it. Afraid it will vanish and prove that what I think I see is just an illusion. Reaching into my purse, I pull out my bell and slowly hold it to the bell on the tree. It looks like a fit! I take the half bell off the tree and push the two jagged pieces together. I suck in my breath. A perfect fit!

A voice behind me gasps, "Bailey!

I whirl around to find the white haired woman standing just inside the door, holding her hands to her heart. For an instant we just stare at each other. I clasp the bell tightly in my hands. Slowly, with halting steps as if she's afraid to step too quickly, else the vision before her eyes will vanish, she comes towards me.

I stare, not certain what to do, for in that moment, I know I'm looking at someone who more than thirty years earlier had packed half of this wooden Christmas bell with a baby girl and sent her to strangers.

"For thirty years I've waited and prayed," she whispered." putting out a trembling hand, then withdrawing it, with uncertainty. "I would know you anywhere." Tears stream down her face. And I don't know what to do, what to say. I think she would like to hug me, but isn't certain how I would react. And I don't know what I would do. "Are you Bailey? Please be Bailey."

"The name on the bell?" I said.

"Yes. Thirty years ago, the bell was separated. Now, it's back in one piece. I've waited all those years for your return," she said, her voice trembling. "Are you called Bailey?"

"Taylor. I'm called Taylor," I said, feeling like I'm in a dream.

She steps closer, reaches out, touches my hair and looks at me as if she does not believe that she's seeing me. Then seeming to be unable to help herself, she folds me in her arms.

"Mother?" Someone said. I look up to see a red headed woman coming towards us. Bradley is standing behind her, staring.

"Oh, Sarah," the woman said, loosing her grip on me, dabbing at her eyes, and reaching out to the young woman. "Come and meet your sister."

Sarah looks at me, disbelief mixed with wonder in her eyes. "Bailey?" Then she is crying and hugging me. "Sister, my sister," she sobs, her face close to my ear. "We knew you would find your way home; we just knew that someday the bell would be complete." I touch the hair, the color of my own, and cannot stop tears from flowing.

We finally stop crying and dab at our eyes with Kleenexes from my purse. A crowd has gathered at the door. Eyes look at us in wonder. A tiny voice from the crowd pipes up, "Don't we get any presents?"

"Come into one of the classrooms," Sarah said. I cling to the bell and numbly let her lead me and the white haired woman into an adjoining room. We all three sit and just stare at each other. I stare at the white haired woman and think, *My Mother! Am I really looking at her? And Sarah? Sister!* Never had I thought about having a real sister.

"Please, can we all just get out of here," the white haired woman said, looking from one to the other of us. Can you come home with us?" She asks, touching a strand of my hair. Then shakes her head and puts a hand to her forehead. "I'm not thinking straight. Of course you must have someone with you. Is your family? Is someone out there waiting and wondering what in the world is going on in here?"

"Friends. I have friends out there," I said.

"Could you come with us?" Sarah asks. "I know we are strangers, but if you've had that half of the bell all your life, then you belong to this family."

"I'll go with you," I hear my own voice say, seeming far

away. I'll go with you, but I need to tell the people I'm with where

I'm going."

"I'll be right back," I said, clutching the bell as I leave the room.

I find Bradley, Hattie and Frank at the table. They look at me, concern and questions on their faces. I know my face is a mess, but I don't care. I lay the bell in front of Bradley. "I found the other half," I say breathlessly."

He stares, wonder in his eyes. "Now, isn't that just astonishing," Hattie said, squeezing my hand.

"Are you going to be all right?" Bradley asked.

"I'm going to be all right," I said. "I'm going to go back to their house with them. There are so many things we need to talk about."

"Sarah Fluty and her mother?" Are you going to Sarah's mother's house?" Bradley asks.

"Yes. I say softly. I think I've found my mother and sister."

Bradley digs into the pocket of his jacket and comes up with a pen, quickly scribbles on a napkin and hands it to me. "My number," he said. "If you need me, I'll be there. I know the place."

"Thanks," I said, more than a little touched by his words. I pick up the bell and numbly go back to the room where my family, lost for thirty years is waiting.

We leave the community building, walk through the snow, and get into Sarah's car and drive to a big green house on Apple Street. Sarah Fluty? My sister is named Sarah Fluty. It's almost as if everything is happening in slow motion. Their voices are saying things like, "I can't believe this. Where have you been? It all seems like a dream."

I feel that it might be in a dream and at any moment I will awaken to find I have only half a bell. I cling to the bell. The women in the front seat. My mother, my sister. I realize I don't know what to call my mother.

Inside the green house on Apple Street, we take off our coats and Sarah says something about coffee. We need coffee. I stare at a beautifully decorated tree in the corner of the room. I walk to the tree and place the bell on it.

We sit on the sofa, me between the two of them, their hands clasping mine.   The bell, in one piece for the first time in thirty years, hangs from a branch on the tree; snow falls softly outside the window; somewhere down the street carolers are singing "Silent Night".

Chapter Nineteen

I listen as this woman, who had given me life, tells me my early history and how it had been after I was no longer a part of her life. "Taylor. Taylor, the woman said, "It is strange to think of you as any name other than Bailey. Yet, I know it must be just as strange to hear yourself referred to other than Taylor."

"Yes. It does sound strange," I said.

We talk into the wee hours of that Christmas Eve morning.

My father had been killed in an automobile accident, my mother seriously injured, in a coma for two weeks, leaving Sarah and me in the care of our mother's parents. Although still very ill, she had come home for a short time just before Christmas that year and had made each child a Christmas bell to hang on the tree, putting the child's name, birth date, and Dell CO on the back of each of the bells.

Then a week before Christmas, my mother started having severe headaches, the doctors said because of the injury she'd suffered in the accident she would have to have brain surgery. Her parents said they would be able to watch Sarah, but couldn't care for two little ones. She had agreed to let the baby be put in foster care, signing what she thought was temporary custody. When she packed my things she had taken the bell from the tree and had impulsively taken it to her father's workshop at the back of the house, sawing it in half. She had placed one half with me in the bassinet that was to go with me and put the other half away, intending for it to be made whole again the next Christmas.

When my mother recovered from the surgery, got back home and demanded that her baby be returned to her, she was shown adoption papers. "I can remember sitting there and wailing, that it was all a mistake, that I hadn't given away my baby. I begged and begged my parents to get you back. They said there was nothing they could do," My mother said, tears again streaming down her face as she remembers, and I am unable to keep my own eyes from filling. Sarah is crying softly, too.

I just sit there and listen as she continues to tell me this incredible story. "I tried to get a lawyer. Not one would take the case. They said I had no case and the papers proved that I had given my child away." She stops and looks at Sarah, reaches over and touches her cheek. "And poor little Sarah, just two years old, had lost her daddy whom she adored, and her mommy was turning into a nut case. And I did, I had a complete breakdown. My parents placed me at the mental hospital over in Sellersville. It took me a year to come out of the breakdown. The doctors said with the stress of losing both my husband and my baby, my mind just closed down.

I still held out hope that somehow, someway, you would return to me; so, on each Christmas I hung your half bell on the tree.

This year Sarah donated the decorations for the tree at the community center, and I agreed to decorate it. At the last minute I took the bell with me and put it on the tree, intending, of course, to take it with me when the celebration was over tonight. It was supposed to be," she said, looking at me in awe. "I'd been out of town and just got back this morning. On impulse, I took the bell with me when I went to decorate at the community center. I shudder to think what if; what if I hadn't put the bell on the tree?" She pauses and just stares at me. "What was your life like?"

"I was well cared for," I tell her.

"Thank God for that. I always tried to imagine you in a big house with parents who adored you. Sometimes, though I'd have a dream, the same dream in which a little girl was needing things and I was too far away to reach her. I looked for you in the face of every little girl who would have been your age. Later when you would have been a teenager, I searched the faces, and when you would have been old enough to attend college. Every time I saw someone with auburn hair, I'd wonder."

She continues, and I just sit there and listen. "Before my world turned upside down, I'd dreamed of having my own shop in Dell and making all sorts of crafts. We lived in Crafton when you were born. And your father fixed me up a little shop in back, and I created all sorts of thing and painted them."

112

"But Dell was on the back of the bell. That's what led me here."

"I put Dell on the back because that's where we were that Christmas, here with my parents."

"I searched in the Dell Tribune from September through December of 1971, looking for a clue; mostly I was looking for anything with Bailey in it. And maybe something about an abandoned baby," I add softly.

"You thought you were abandoned?"

"I didn't know. I though it might have been the case."

"I want you to know I never intended to abandon you; my babies were everything to me."

"I know you didn't," I said, wanting to say something to ease her pain, knowing that words won't help, and even time wouldn't heal.

"Bradley West had a picture of Sarah when she was seven," I said. "In it with her were a couple and two other women. On the back it named one of the women as Aunt Rett."

"I have a copy," Sarah said, getting up from the couch, going into an adjoining room. She hurries back with an envelope. "I make copies of any picture I let anyone take," she said, sitting down. She dumps out snapshots and picks up one. "Here, is this the one?" She hands it to me.

I take it. It is identical to the one Bradley had. "That is Sarah when she was seven," my mother said, and this is me," she said, pointing to the white headed woman.

"You had white hair back then?"

"Yes. Just after I found out you were gone and I couldn't get you back, my hair turned white in a span of two months. I once had hair the color of yours and Sarah's." She shakes her head and continues to name the people in the picture. "These two were my parents. I was adopted, too," she said softly, squeezing my hand. "I know what it's like to ask and be told you don't need to know."

"Did you ever find out who your birth parents were?"

"No," she said. "I asked my parents many times, even though they got angry. They said I shouldn't ask, that it didn't matter." She looks into my eyes. "It mattered," she said, a catch in her voice. "It mattered so very, very much. And when I thought about my own child out there asking the same questions I'd asked and maybe not getting any answers, it just tore my heart to shreds."

Sarah put an arm around her mother's shoulder and laid her head against hers. After a moment, she raises her head and looks at me. "This is all so incredible. It is almost like a dream." She said. And with tears glistening in her eyes, said, "Sister. I have my sister sitting close enough to touch. After all those years of only having four pictures of you, I have a flesh and bones sister."

I think it must have been very painful for her growing up wondering about a lost sister and her mom being filled with sadness for that lost child. It looked like we all had lost a great deal.

I look at the picture again. That woman? Aunt Rett? My grandmother? "Just who is this woman in the snapshot?" I ask, pointing to the woman in the picture. You call her Aunt Rett. Was she one of your parents' sister?"

"No," my mother said, taking the picture and studying the faces. "Aunt Rett was....," she hesitates, as if she can't find the words to describe the woman in the picture. "Aunt Rett was sorta like a shadow."

"What do you mean?"

"She came in and out of our lives once a year. She'd stand in the background, almost like she was a camera recording everything. I can't remember her ever saying much to me. But she did have lengthy conversations behind closed doors with my parents. And when she was gone they never spoke of her. As I look back, it was strange."

"I think I know.... I knew the woman in the picture," I said breathlessly.

"You knew Aunt Rett?" They ask in unison, looking at me in astonishment.

"She was my grandmother."

"That's amazing," Sarah said. "How can that be? But you know when we finally know all there is to know, it will all fit together like a puzzle and we'll be able to look back and say, of course, it all fits."

Like two pieces of a Christmas bell.

"Then if Aunt Rett and your grandmother were one and the same then she knew where you were; she knew that I was desperately seeking my daughter," my mother said, her voice quivering. "But why did she keep coming back here? I never felt that she was a close friend of my parents, in fact, although they never talked about her, I sensed that they dreaded her visits. What was the connection? She left our lives when Sarah was ten; you would have been eight. My parents said Aunt Rett died. No one ever mentioned her again."

"My grandmother died when I was eight."

"If she is the same person, how's it all tied together?" Sarah asks.

Our mother looks from me to Sarah, "You know I've wondered countless times where our red hair came from. Who gave it to us? Do we have Irish ancestors? I was born in 1949. I wish someone had left a clue."

Suddenly something Aunt Kate had said floats across my mind, *Mother Winfield went to Colorado in 1949, leaving her boys.* "You were born in 1949?"

"I was. My mother did tell me that much. I was born in a little town just outside Denver on July 12, 1949, but she swore that was all she knew."

"Grandmother Winfield spent the summer of 1949 in Colorado," I said softly. "My Aunt Kate told me. She said Grandmother left her boys for the whole summer of that year."

"It is all connected," my mother said. "It all has to be connected someway. Aunt Rett. Your grandmother. One and the same, holding the secret to it all. If we only had the keys to the secret. Mama muttered that word for several days before she died. She repeated over and over again, 'Secrets. Secrets, it's all in the secrets.' The doctor said she was talking out of her head. But I wonder if she was trying to tell me something."

"Grandma's novel!" Sarah screams, jumping to her feet. "I hadn't thought about this in years. Remember," Sarah said, excitement shining in her large, green eyes, grabbing her mother's hands in hers. "Remember when I was fourteen and Grandma caught me going through that old trunk in the attic. Remember how upset she was that I was snooping into her personal papers?"

"Yes, I do remember that. You were grounded for two weeks."

"What I never told you was what I found. What I found so intriguing in that trunk was a novel. A handwritten novel Grandma had written called "Secrets"."

She stares at Sarah in astonishment, "Mama wrote a novel! I never knew. And she called it Secrets? Could that be what she was talking about, there at the end when she was so sick?"

Sarah continues to tell us about the novel. "It was about a woman who came and visited a family once a year, and she had total control over the family."

I sit there and look at these two: One who just until today had only been a dream, a longing, and the other one, this sister, who until today hadn't even been a dream, and I listen as they talk between them and it is like they are slowly unraveling secrets that revealed all our life's history. I feel a chill creep across my shoulders at the wonder of it all and pinch the inside of my lower arm just to know I'm not in a dream myself.

"I think it was all there in that novel, Mama! I didn't get to read all of it, but I remember the title was "Secrets". It said novel, but now that I think about it, it read like a journal. I remember it so clearly, it was handwritten on typing paper, both sides, then she had bound it in a brown binder." Sarah closes her eyes as if she's seeing again what a fourteen-year-old had seen. "I can see it clearly, on the binding was printed in large letters, "Secrets" a novel, by Emma Roland. It was all about a woman who let a couple adopt her daughter, born of an affair. Then she controlled the family from afar."

Sarah opens her eyes and looks from her mother to me. "I don't think Grandma ever knew I'd found the novel. But I think she thought I'd come close. She'd hidden it underneath the cardboard that lined the top of the lid. I only noticed it because one end of the cardboard was loose. I went there to the trunk five or six afternoon after school. The words in the writing were powerful and seemed to just keep pulling me back. Each day, I couldn't wait to get home and find out more. I was just about half way through when Grandma caught me in the trunk. When I heard her on the steps, I'd managed to slip the manuscript back beneath the cardboard, but she caught me before I could close the lid. I'd never seen her so angry. Then you made me promise never to touch that trunk again. You didn't have to worry; Grandma put a padlock on it. I never told you about what I'd found. I never dreamed it was about the family."

My mother suddenly springs off the couch and stands before us, the fingers on her right hand trembles against her lips. "I still have Mama's trunk," she whispered.

"Do you think the novel is still behind the cardboard after all this time?" Sarah asks. "I didn't know you got the trunk. I thought everything was sold before she went into the nursing home."

"It was. Everything but the trunk. It was so beat up that no one would have bid on it at the auction anyway. It still had the padlock on it. I pried it off with a crowbar. All that was in it was some old tax records and a quilt she'd made. I brought it home, a link to home, I guess. Perhaps we all need that."

"Where's the trunk now, Mama," Sarah said, grabbing her mother's arms.

"In the attic. It's still in the attic."

They stare at each other for a few seconds, then say in unison, "Come on!" My mother looks back at me, "Come on!"

I think this whole episode with the woman's novel and her last words, whispered, is eerily like what happened between me and my mother when she lay dying.

Sarah is already out of sight, going up the stairs. I followed close behind my mother as she quickly went up the stairs, thinking that even Libby would have a hard time believing all that has happened this one special Christmas season.

Soon all three of us are in the attic. A lone light bulb, suspended from a rafter, illuminated the room, which is filled with boxes and broken, old furniture, pieces of lives lived, much like the attic I'd sat in just days ago when I'd found the bell.

"It's over here someplace," my mother said, pulling aside cardboard boxes of various sizes.

Sarah grabs boxes, tossing them aside. I watch, not yet feeling comfortable enough, not yet familiar enough with these two that years and circumstances have bonded together. And the same years and circumstances have left me a giant gap too wide to allow me to join in. As I stand there and watch the two of them working together, I realize there is so much I'll never have, that it's impossible to ever get back what was never built. I feel a great loss as I watch the two of them, yet I know with what I've found this Christmas season, my cup is more than overflowing.

"Here it is!" Sarah said, yanking at a beat-up looking brown trunk.

My mother grabs a leather strap and helps Sarah pull the trunk into the middle of the room.

Sarah flips open the lid, then hesitates and steps back a step. "You see if it's there, Mama."

Sarah puts an arm around my shoulder as we watch, holding our breaths, as our mother finally flings back the cardboard. A tatted brown folder falls into the trunk.

Chapter Twenty

Our mother picks up the folder, turns and looks at us. "I'm almost afraid to look inside, afraid I won't find the answers to questions I've wondered about all my life."

For a moment there is silence in the attic.

"Come," she said, hugging the folder to her chest. "Let's go downstairs, fix hot chocolate and read."

And so we did. We sat in the living room of my birth mother's house in Dell Colorado, on a night that had, I suppose, turned to Christmas Eve at the stroke of midnight. We sat, the three of us on the couch, the fire crackling and sending gold and red shadows over the tree, on which amidst all the other beautiful decoration hangs one red bell, complete for the first time since that Christmas season thirty years ago. We sat there, and my mother's voice read, from the yellowed pages of a manuscript, filling the house with truths she'd waited a lifetime to know.

Chapter Twenty-one

As she read about those people, whose identity had been changed with a name and a place, she'd pause, catching her breath with some new discovery she'd thought lost to her forever. As I watched her read, I knew exactly how she felt.

We learned that Aunt Rett was indeed Grandmother Winfield. That she was in reality my birth mother's mother. In the novel her name was Loraine Fields. She'd come from a small town in Illinois, which for some reason the author had chosen to call "Paradise", to Dell Colorado because she was going to have a baby and must, at all cost, keep it a secret.

From the pages of the novel we learned that in late 1948, when Loraine's husband was in Europe,---just like my grandfather, she'd had an affair with a dashing, auburn haired man named Samuel Duncan. She'd faked a breakdown and had gone to Denver Colorado where she had a good friend from her college days. But when she got there she found that the friend was very ill and she never told the friend about her dilemma. She met a maid at the hotel she was staying at. "Mama!" my mother exclaims, laying the folder down on her lap and looking at us. "Mama worked at a hotel when she was first married. In fact, both Mama and Daddy worked there the first few years of their marriage. She told me that."

"Please read on," Sarah said.

As she resumed reading, we learned that Loraine made a deal with the young couple in the novel. They'd adopt her child, whom she named Rosealee; she'd give them a nice house somewhere in a small town; she'd visit once a year, and under no circumstances would her secret ever be revealed. The young couple had agreed to the deal, had sworn on a Bible never to break the promise.

The narrator of the novel, who both my mother and Sarah readily identify as their mother and grandmother, was named Tess. Tess came to despise Loraine and wanted to stop her yearly visits. Wanted to get her out of their lives forever, but Loraine told the couple if they ever tried to get away from her she would find them, that she would destroy them, that she had the resources to do so. They did not doubt her and lived in fear of her. All they could do, the novel said was hate, hate, hate.

My mother laid the manuscript on her lap, rubbed her eyes, and said, "Looking back now, I can see the hate in Mama's eyes every time Aunt Rett came. She brought me things, clothes. She never gave them to me herself, and after she was gone Mama would drag out a sack full of new clothes. I don't remember her ever bringing me a toy. Just clothes."

I stare at the manuscript and remember Boo. And the teddy bear that was, as far as I knew, still on the shelf in the house in Scalesville.

My mother reads on. Tess and her husband tolerate the yearly visits of Loraine. Rosealee marries a young man Tess doesn't approve of. "That was a fact for sure," My mother said, looking from Sarah to me. "She never liked your father."

"What was his name?" I ask.

My mother reaches over and squeezes my hand. "His name was Stanley Eugene Fleeming," she said softly. "He was a good man and a loving father.

"You're tired, Mama," Sarah said. "Want me to read awhile?"

"No, honey. I want to read it, every word. I just need a break. It's three o'clock," she said, looking at her watch. "Are you ok, honey?" she asks, looking at me. "So much has happened. How can we absorb it all? Yet, I feel I can't stop until every word in the novel is read; every secret revealed."

"I'm doing fine," I tell her, knowing that I want just as much as she does to know every secret.

My mother picks up the manuscript and begins reading again. She reads. "It was the fall of 1971 and Rosealee had given birth to a second child, a girl named Ashley." She pauses and looks at me. We both knew that the baby was me. "It's all so autobiographical," my mother said in amazement.

"It's just like you're reading from the pages of our lives," Sarah said. "The only difference is that we are looking into Grandma's thoughts. We are actually seeing what she was feeling and thinking. I'm beginning to see her in a whole new light."

Our mother's voice trembles as she reads about Rosealee being in an accident in which she was seriously injured, her husband killed.

Loraine came to visit, took charge of the situation and insisted that Tess have Rosealee give up the baby. Loraine would take the baby, she knew someone who would adopt her. Tess said Rosealee would never do that. But they told Rosealee she would be giving the baby up temporarily. She signed the papers, thinking that just as soon as she was well enough, the baby would be returned. Our mother pauses, tears streaming down her face. Sarah hugs her.

She reads on about the baby leaving, but no mention of a bell. "She didn't mention the bell," I said.

"Mama didn't know about me putting the bell inside your blanket. I put my half of the bell away. Mama didn't know about it, until a few years later when she asked about the half bell hanging on my tree."

She reads about Rosealee having a breakdown. Tears stream down her face in remembrance.

The manuscript ends in 1978. My mother reads, " Loraine died today. The family is free."

My mother closes the manuscript. "I wondered about my birth mother since I found out I was adopted, now to discover at age fifty that she was in and out of my life and yet I never knew her, never knew her at all. But as sad as this makes me feel, the knowing is worth it. And to know I got my red hair from someone makes me feel I have roots, not just hanging out there in mid air somewhere."

I swallow hard. I know. I know exactly what she's talking about.

I look at these two people, strangers, yet so much a part of me and wonder if I'll wake up at any moment and it will all be a dream.

"Look, look girls," my mother said as the first gray of morning light came through the window. It's Christmas Eve. It's the most extraordinary Christmas Eve."

And we stand there, this mother and two daughters, one on each side of her, their heads on her shoulders, her arm around each and look towards the East. The sky shifts from the gray of dawn to a faint pink then slowly turns rosy, then rays of sunlight burst forth, casting gold on the new fallen snow.

As I stand there in the circle of my mother's arm, I feel both happy and sad. Happy that I've finally found this person who gave me the gift of life, and a sister yet to know. And the sadness is for the years lost with these two; sadness for the memories I wasn't here to record. It's like a blank slate in some part of my mind; a blank slate that no future days can ever write, for that slate, those pages of my life will always remain blank.

"Merry Christmas, my daughters," our mother said, kissing us both on the cheek.

"Merry Christmas, Mama. Merry Christmas, Bailey,... Taylor, " Sarah said.

"Merry Christmas," I said, I don't feel comfortable calling my mother Mama. I don't know what to call her.

She looks at me and smiles. "We have time. We have time." I look into her eyes and see the understanding there. "Come on, let's get that coffee."

We fill our cups with coffee. "Come into the living room next to the tree," my mother said.

She excuses herself and goes into another room.

Sarah sits beside me. "Our first Christmas. You know, although I couldn't remember you, I always felt cheated especially at this time of year. I always thought someone had taken something precious out of my life, and they had. I wanted you here when I first rode a bike, when I learned to swim, when I had my first crush on a boy, when I had my first broken heart. I wanted my sister to tell it all to."

I look at her, this woman who was my big sister, a woman I don't know, but want to so desperately. I hug her. "We can go from here," is all I know to say.

Our mother comes back into the room. "Open this. These are for you." She hands me an envelope, inside are four pictures. I'm seeing in photographs the first months of my life: A wailing baby, looking just hours old; A proud little sister with her newborn prize; A father smiling, looking down on a bundle in his arms. I stare at his face. A face I'll never look at, never build a memory with. I swallow hard, and move on to the next picture: one of a young woman holding a wide-eyed baby. "Thanks," is all I can say.

We sit and talk until the sun is filling the room. They want to know everything there is to know about me, and I tell them.

And they tell me about themselves. "Sarah's work is sold all over the country," our mother says proudly. "Big wedding three years ago. Owen Fluty is a special young man."

"I left him in New York. He was supposed to catch a later flight. An ice storm hit suddenly, and the plane couldn't leave. He thinks he'll be in on a 4 p.m. flight." Sarah's lower lip quivers. "I don't want to even consider that he wouldn't be with me on Christmas."

"He'll be here, honey. Don't you worry," our mother said.

I suddenly feel so tired, my body and mind numb. I feel the need to be alone, to gather my thoughts and try to sort out all that has transpired in the last few hours. I want to go back to my room at Hattie's.

I don't know just how to tell them, I want to be by myself, that I need to be just by myself, that I have to be by myself. So, I decided to just tell them the truth. "I'm going to go back to the Bed and Breakfast," I tell them, hoping they will understand. "I need to be alone; to try to sort out all that has been revealed in the past few hours."

My mother looks at me for a long moment. I look back at her, trying to read her face. Do I see hurt? Understanding? I hope for understanding. She nods. "I understand." And I feel that she really does, that she knows I have my way of dealing with life's situations that she has no knowledge of. "You will return soon?"

"Soon," I said.

"It's all right" she said. "You need your time alone. Do what you need to do and come back to us."

I ask to use the phone and dial the number Bradley West had scribbled on the napkin. "This is Taylor. Can you come and get me?"

"I'm on my way."

As I put on my coat and boots, my mother tells me words, words all mothers say, words mothers should say, "Be careful. Make that young man drive safely." She hugs me, whispers, "Love you."

Sarah hugs me and says, "You'll be back," as if she's afraid I'll just walk out the door and that will be it, her little sister lost again.

"I'll be back," I say, hugging her tightly.

"Come to church tonight. Meet us at the church," Sarah said.

"Come and welcome Christmas with us. We'll be there for the midnight service," Our mother said. "If you don't make it back here before that, meet us there. It's the Free Will Church on Huntington Avenue."

"I've heard about the service. I'll be there."

Bradley's car is pulling into the drive. By the time I get the door open and am out on the porch, he's already out of the car and headed towards me. "Thanks for coming," I said.

"Are you ok?" he asks, putting an arm around my waist.

"Yes. Yes, I'm ok."

When we are in the car and start to pull away, I look back towards the house. My mother and sister wave from the open door.

Chapter Twenty-two

Bradley drives slowly back to Hattie's. "Are you all right?" He asks, squeezing my shoulder.

"It is all so unbelievable," I tell him.

We drive in silence then. I sense that he knows I need the silence. I look at the beautiful lawns of the large houses, all covered in a winter wonderland. Families inside. I just left my mother whom I'd dreamed of meeting since I was eight, and a sister who I'd just discovered. But the need to just be alone had been so great that I'd had to leave. What was that old saying, *"You can't go home again."* As we pull into Hattie's driveway, I think I understand that saying. I think it's about things lost and that you just have to let it be and don't go trying to fill up an old jar; that you have to find and try to fill a new jar.

Bradley pulls as close as he can get to Hattie's front door. He hadn't asked questions, although I knew he was filled with them. It was as if he knew I needed the quiet. He starts to get out, "I'll see you to the door."

I put my hand on his arm. "No. I'll be ok. Thanks so much for coming to pick me up."

"It was what I wanted to do."

"I'll tell you later what went on in that house on Apple Street."

He lays his gloved hand over mine. "There will be time," he said, looking into my eyes.

I get out of the car, shut the door and begin walking towards Hattie's porch.

I step into the warm foyer. Before I push the door to behind me, I look toward the driveway. Bradley's car is still sitting there.

"You all right, Taylor?" Hattie asks, coming into the room.

"I'm fine," I tell her and stoop to hug Scottie, who is thumping his tail against my leg.

"Would you like anything to eat?" Hattie offers. And I think that she'd like to know what I'd learned in the hours I'd been gone.

"No, thanks, Hattie. I just want to get to bed for a few hours.

"You go right ahead, honey."

I hurry up the stairs. Inside my room I take off my coat and boots and just fall across the bed, both mentally and physically exhausted. I reach for my coat lying on the chair next to the bed and pull the pictures out of the pocket, tucking them beneath the pillow, then I crawl, with my clothes still on, beneath the quilts. I feel myself drifting with visions of my mother fitting back together a jagged edged Christmas bell. I see Sarah as a two-year-old smiling at a baby sister, and I see Bradley West making his way to my heart's door. And I see myself standing on the edge of it all, wondering if I dared to belong to any of it.

Chapter Twenty-three

I awaken. For a moment I don't know where I'm at. Then I realize that I'm in the bed in my room at Hattie's place in Dell Colorado. It's dark. I wonder what time it is? I pull myself up onto my elbow and reach for my watch on the nightstand, I don't remember taking it off. Eight o'clock. I'd been asleep for hours. I'd come back here to try to sort out my thoughts and all I had done was sleep.

I get out of bed, go to the window and look out. Snow is falling again. Beautiful large flakes drift to the already covered ground. The evergreens in front of Bradley's cottage are covered. The cottage is dark. I wonder where he is? I shower, blow dry my hair, put on a bit of makeup and dress in my best gray slacks and matching sweater. I hear a knock on the door and open it to find Hattie standing there. "Just seeing if you need anything," she said.

I tell her I'm fine.

"Did you see that it's snowing again?" she asks.

"I did. It's so beautiful."

"I love a white Christmas," she said, then added. "Supper is on the stove. Frank and I are going out for awhile, visiting an old friend. Then we'll visit his sister. When you are ready, just go on down and help yourself. Bradley is working in the den."

"Thanks Hattie," I said, hugging her. "Thanks so much for everything.

She hugs me back. "Well, Frank is waiting in the car for me. We'll see you later. You are coming to the midnight service at the church?"

"Yes. I'll be there."

"Want us to come back and get you to go with us?"

"No. I can drive myself. I found them, Hattie. I found my mother and sister. They will be at the church."

"Praise the Lord!" Hattie said, hugging me again. "It's all

so amazing. Is there anything I can do for you?"

"No. But thanks so much for all your kindness to me."

"You are a wonderful young lady. I feel honored that the Lord saw fit to send you my way this Christmas season." She gives me another hug. "See you at the church. We'll have a long talk when you're ready."

When her footsteps on the stairs are silent, I go down the stairs and into the kitchen. A stew is still warm on the stove and fresh baked bread is on a board nearby. I get a bowl and ladle out a generous helping, slice off a piece of the bread and carry it to the white and yellow checkered table.

I wonder if Bradley is still in the den working on his book? Has he eaten? I know I'm just giving myself excuses to go to the den and see if he's there. I find him bending over the table, putting photographs with pages of print. I rap on the doorframe. He looks up with a smile that tells me he's glad to see me.

"Would you like something to eat? Hattie left plenty of stew. I'm getting ready to eat right now."

"Sounds good to me," he said.

Back in the kitchen, he fills a bowl with stew, cuts off a king sized hunk of bread, goes to the refrigerator, finds the butter dish and brings it all to the table.

I feel that he has dozens of questions and I want to tell him. He looks at me over his coffee cup.

"My mother, my biological mother, had the other half of my bell," I tell him."

"So you found what you came to Dell to find?"

"Yes. I found the other half of the bell, my birth mother, a sister, and enough about my family that would fill one of your novels."

"Are you ok with what you found?" He asked, looking closely at me, his eyes filled with concern.

"Yes. I'm ok with what I found, but I'm having a hard time trying to consume all the information." We sit there in silence for a moment, then I begin telling my inner thoughts to this man, this stranger, yet I don't feel he's a stranger, my heart tells me that I'm comfortable with him, that I trust him. I'm listening to that little voice Libby said to always listen to. And I sit there in Hattie's sunny kitchen and open my soul to this man, spilling out the part of me that would have a few days ago said, don't let another see the deepest part of you.

And the dark-eyed man sitting across from me listens as I talk. I tell him how I didn't know how to feel about my mother, that I'm troubled by not feeling instant love for her. Where was that bond between mother and child? Bradley takes my hands in his. "How could you feel such a bond, you just met her? But you have time, Taylor. Time to form a bond. Maybe it won't be the same as it would have been had you known your mother your whole life, but you can build from this day. You can build from this day."

"I'm going to meet my mother and sister for the services at the Free Will Church tonight. Would you go with me?"

"I would love to go with you."

He looks at his watch. "It's getting late; I'd better go to the cottage and get cleaned up. What time do you want me to pick you up?"

"The service is at midnight. I would like to be there about a quarter til."

"I'll pick you up at eleven-thirty."

"I'll be ready."

I stand in the doorway and watch him walk to the cottage. Church with Bradley West, my mother and sister on Christmas Eve seems fitting.

Chapter Twenty-four

When Bradley comes to the door, I get my coat, and he holds it while I slip my arms into the sleeves. Snowflakes cling to his overcoat and hair. Outside, he slips my arm through his as we walk towards his car. Everything is so quiet, so white, so beautiful.

With his hand on the handle of the door to the passenger side of the car, Bradley pauses, snow collecting in his hair, and looks at me. "I've been thinking about the story of your Christmas bell and when I get the novel that I'm working on now, written, I'd like to try to write one based on it."

"You would?" I said, not able to think of anything else to say. He opens the door and I slide into the seat. He closes the door, goes around to the driver's side and gets in.

He starts the engine and backs up. I'm still thinking about what he'd said about wanting to write a novel about my bell, wondering what ending he'd write? Happy? Sad? I hope he would write it happy. "I'd like to read some of your work," I tell him as he pulls the car onto the street.

He looks at me and smiles. "I'd like that very much."

I look at the snow-covered shops as he drives slowly down the deserted streets of Dell. "It's all so beautiful," I said.

"Ah," Bradley said, "There is no place like Dell at Christmas time. It has a sorta magic, if you know what I mean."

"I know," I said softly. "I know."

When we get to the parking lot of the church, a few cars are already there. The church is small; a brown brick with stained glass windows from which a soft light shines. A high steeple shoots into the sky. "What a charming little church," I said.

"It is beautiful," Bradley said, turning to me, making no attempt to get out of the car. "What are your plans, Taylor?"

"Well, I have to get back to my job in Cincinnati. They will be replacing me if I don't show up when the school term begins after the first of the year."

He leans towards me and gently runs his fingers down my face. "You are very special, Taylor Winfield," he said huskily, his face so close I can feel his breath, smell the faint scent of Old Spice, and then he brushes his lips across mine. "I hope you will not be a stranger to Dell Colorado."

I just stare at him, feeling a tingle clear to my toes. I want to lay my head on his shoulder, feel myself wrapped in his strong arms. Libby would say that it is happening, the magic is happening. "We'd better go in," I heard myself say.

We walk to the door and Bradley pushes it open. My mother is sitting on a bench just inside the vestibule. She gets up and rushes to hug me. "I'm so glad you are here."

"Hello, Mr. West," she said, taking his outstretched hand.

"It's good to see you again, Ms. Fleeming."

Sarah's red head pops around the door of the wide archway. She smiles and hurries towards me, pulling on the hand of a tall, lanky, blonde haired man. She hugs me. "This is Owen Fluty, my husband," she said, looking at the man as if he's someone extra special. Hadn't I seen that look when Bradley had looked at me in the car?

Owen clasps my hand in both his huge ones. "I'm so glad to finally meet you. My Sarah is so happy to have you back in her life."

"Come," my mother said, getting on one side of me and looping her other arm through Sarah's. Bradley West walks beside me into the sanctuary. There is a stillness here, a hushed quietness, I think we are all feeling the awe. The pews glisten a rich mahogany, from the light of the old-fashioned globe lanterns on the walls. Several people are already seated. We sit three rows from the front. I sit between my mother and Bradley, and Sarah and Owen sit to her left. From somewhere, "Silent Night" is softly playing.

I look about the room; A young couple sit with two little girls between them. Near the back is a teenaged boy with long stringy hair. An old couple hold hands. To the left and down a bit sit Hattie and Frank. They wave. I smile at them, glad they are here.

The minister, a man who appears to be in his forties, walks to the pulpit. He is dressed in a flowing white robe with a yellow sash across his shoulders. He smiles. "Welcome," he begins. "It is wonderful to be here in God's house on this Christmas Eve. Let us stand and join together in prayer."

Everyone stands and bows their heads as he begins to pray. "Bless each and every one of those who have gathered here in your house, Lord. We thank you for all your blessings this Holiday season; we thank you for giving us your greatest gift, your son. In Jesus' name amen."

The minister tells the age-old Christmas story. I find that my hand is being held in the hand of Bradley West and I leave it there. It feels right being there. My mother smiles at me, making me feel she is glad I found my way home. My sister reaches across our mother and pats my hand.

It is like being in one of Libby's Fairy Tales, being here with these people, who are so rapidly becoming a part of my life. I look at Bradley, and he smiles at me, causing my heart to do that flip again. One Christmas, two Christmases from now will he be in my life? My mother is close enough that I can feel the warmth of her body. I believe she will be in my life for all the Christmases we have left in which both of us are in this world. And Sarah? My sister. How strange to think that I have a sister. As we go down the road of life, I think we will become not only sisters, but also best friends. And as she and Owen continue their life together, possibly nieces and nephews on the horizon, faces not yet in this world coming someday to light it up even brighter than it already is. And Hattie? Dear Hattie. Without her taking me in, I would have just gone on to the next town and tried to find a motel. Without her, I may have never found Bradley West, or my mother and sister. As Libby would say, *"It's all meant to be, Taylor. It's all in the scheme of things. If you believe and listen to your little voice, you'll find just how it was planned all along."*

133

And maybe she's right; maybe a higher power is at work and we just have to tune in. One thing I know is true: It feels right, being here with these people, in this little church on this Christmas Eve. It feels like family. It feels like home.

To order copies of "The Christmas Bell".

Send check or money order for $15.00
(this includes shipping and handling.) to:
Cedar Hill Press
P.O. Box 235
Knightstown, IN 46148